leisure &

Smugglers' Fox

Also by
SUSANNA BAILEY

Praise for *Snow Foal*

'I absolutely love *Snow Foal* – it's so truthful, tender and touching. A book to read in a day and remember for a lifetime.' Dame Jacqueline Wilson, author of the Tracy Beaker books

'How much my daughter and I enjoyed *Snow Foal*! It's a gripping, sensitively written book.' Jenny McLachlan, author of *The Land of Roar*

'A mesmerising new voice about a girl that deserves to be heard.' Joanna Nadin

'One of my most highly-anticipated reads of the year.' Hana Tooke, author of *The Unadoptables*

'A tender, lyrical tale for a cold winter's night that will lift the spirits and warm the heart.' Steve Voake

Praise for *Otters' Moon*

'A beautiful story, immersed in the wild and restorative power of nature. I loved it.' Gill Lewis, author of *Sky Hawk*

'Sue writes with sensitivity and understanding about two children struggling to navigate complex emotions and situations.' Julia Green

'An excellent book – haunting and lovely. A delightful work of art.' Anthony McGowan

Praise for *Raven Winter*

'This is such a sensitive and beautiful story. Difficult themes are handled with a deft touch without sacrificing realism, and the relationship between Billie and her bird is so tenderly drawn. It's brilliant.' – Katya Balen

'I loved Raven Winter. Full of empathy and compassion, this beautifully written story sensitively addresses issues of coercive control and domestic and emotional abuse. With themes of friendship, family, kindness and the healing power of nature, this is a great read.' Kevin Cobane, Empathy Lab judge, VIP Reading and teacher

Smugglers' Fox

SUSANNA BAILEY

First published in Great Britain in 2023 by Farshore

An imprint of HarperCollins*Publishers*
1 London Bridge Street, London SE1 9GF

farshore.co.uk

HarperCollins*Publishers*
Macken House, 39/40 Mayor Street Upper,
Dublin 1, D01 C9W8

Text copyright © 2023 Susanna Bailey

The moral rights of the author have been asserted

A CIP catalogue record of this title is available from the British Library

ISBN 978 1 4052 9998 5

Printed and bound in the UK using 100% renewable electricity at
CPI Group (UK) Ltd

1

Typeset by Avon DataSet Ltd, Alcester, Warwickshire

Chapter heads and text break artwork © Shutterstock

Stay safe online. Any website addresses listed in this book are correct at the
time of going to print. However, Farshore is not responsible for content
hosted by third parties. Please be aware that online content can be subject to
change and websites can contain content that is unsuitable for children. We
advise that all children are supervised when using the internet.

This book is produced from independently certified FSC™ paper
to ensure responsible forest management.

For more information visit: www.harpercollins.co.uk/green

For my gorgeous grandchildren:
Luca, Jules, and Valentina.

And in memory of my lovely,
lovely friend, Giles Williams.

"You would imagine any man mad, from all that you see around you, who would think of trusting himself to the ocean."

Charles Dickens, while touring the graveyards of the Yorkshire coast in 1851 . . .

# PROLOGUE

The young fox caught the scent and sounds long before she spotted their source. She froze. What, or who, was coming through the hedge; their movements travelling through the wet ground towards her, trembling through her body?

Was it him? The man with the stick that beat the ground, the net that swept the air and reached for her? She hunched low, peered around the corner of the shed. She waited; eyes narrow, front paw raised in readiness for escape.

No. Not Net-and-Stick-Man. His scent was bitter on the air, his tread heavier. And it wasn't the smaller human that picked his way on the shore like the beach birds. His sounds were soft, careful, less urgent than these new ones. And the scent of Beach-Bird-Boy was kinder, salty, wrapped within it, always the drift of woodsmoke – and food.

The hedge crackled and shook. Whoever was coming through thrashed and kicked as they went now, so that a smog rose in the fox's sensitive nostrils, as if the earth was now air instead of ground. She flicked out her tongue, tasted rain and the bitter nip of leaves ripped from their woody stems, the spicy bleed of sap.

No. This was not the man she feared nor the boy she knew. But this was human scent. A scent the fox's mother had taught her to fear, to run from. Even now, she kept her distance from Beach-Bird-Boy, lured only by the burn of her empty stomach; the hope of the sometimes scraps of his meal on the cave floor.

Adrenaline quivered in her limbs. She glanced over her shoulder, back towards her shortcut to safety. The squeeze-tight rock-space that led down to the darkness of the sand-strewn cave and, should she need it, the drip-drip musty darkness of the tunnels beyond. She measured the distance in her mind, tensed for the swift twist and dart that would take her out of danger in seconds.

Suddenly, nothing.

All was still. Quiet.

Then a thin sound threaded the air. It pulled at the fox, stirred something within her. A memory. Or a knowledge carried in her bones from somewhere else, somewhere before her time. She rose a little higher on her haunches, pushed her nose forward past the damp shed wall that hid her. Sniffed. Stared.

She knew this scent. This was the other small human.

The one that threw down warm, meaty food that left salted fat on her whiskers.

The one that smelled of fear.

She tipped her head to one side. Watched him out of the corner of one golden eye. Why was he there, curled in a ball like the thorn-backed hedgehogs she had learned to leave alone? Rocking slightly, like a young tree in the wind and rain. Sniffling and snuffling, sick, perhaps.

The fox moved forward, just an inch. Curious now; sure of an easy escape, doubtful of any threat.

The hedgehog-human uncurled and crawled from the hedge. It lifted its head, turned her way. Twists of hair, black as old seaweed. Night-dark eyes, round and wet as sea-washed pebbles, staring into her own. She'd been right that first time. Hedgehog-Boy was no threat.

She pushed her nose forward, sniffed again. No scent of blood. But he was wounded somehow . . .

And all alone, just like her.

CHAPTER 1
BEFORE

Mam took a whole month deciding what to call me and my brother. 'Because names, they're important, Jonah. They say something about who you are.'

Turned out she was right, only in my case, not in the way she thought.

According to Mam (and Google) Jonah means 'dove'. Doves, Mam said, are all about 'peace' and 'love' and 'new life'. And that was how she felt when I was born: peaceful and fizzing with love, all at the same time. Like holding me made everything new. Made *her* new.

It didn't, though.

I didn't.

I found out that lots of people around the world think the name Jonah is bad luck, because of a legend about a Jonah who was swallowed by a whale. Which is *very* bad luck, whichever way you look at it.

That's the kind of Jonah I am. The bad-luck kind.

Mam chose well, just for the wrong reasons.

She called my little brother Rio, after a place called Rio de Janeiro, 'where people party in the streets all day like brightly feathered birds, and the sun shines the whole time, even in winter'.

Mam got his name right too. But in a good way. Rio's *made* of sunshine. He makes people happy. Or he used to. I haven't seen Rio's bright colours for a while now, not since – everything.

Mam's name is Sarah. Well, that's her real name anyway. It was written on a piece of paper, pinned to a yellow baby blanket, when she was found – left in a box, tucked between sand dunes and seagulls on Redcar beach. Those are the only two things she knows about herself for sure. So maybe that's why she thinks names are important. Except it can't be, because she doesn't use that name any more. She calls herself Marina, which means 'from the sea'. 'Because I was,' she says.

Maybe she's right. And maybe it came back for her that last day in Whitby, and that's why she's vanished into thin air.

CHAPTER 2
BEFORE

I had a weird feeling about our visit with Mam. The feeling got worse when Jo, our foster carer, said Mam wanted to meet in Whitby – a seaside place famous for storms and shipwrecks. And Dracula.

Mam was 'definitely' coming this time. Our social worker had called on her that morning, to check. So that was *something*. But my heart jumped around like an anxious bird as the clock ticked round towards 'early lunch' before setting off for Whitby. Because with Mam you never knew anything for certain.

And because when she *did* turn up to see us, she always had to leave again. Then it was like someone took the lid off a jar full of wasps, one that you'd tightened and tightened until your face went hot, but wouldn't fit back on again. The wasps swarmed around your head; followed you wherever you went for days and days, stinging. Stinging. Until you found a new lid.

I glanced at the clock. 10.45. Ages to go.

3

Rio was in busy-bee mode, 'helping' Jo tidy his room. His feet made tiny thunderstorms on the ceiling above the sitting room. How much did *he* remember about Mam's other 'visits' – the ones when she didn't turn up? The ones where she did, but hardly seemed to notice that *we* had? Hard to know. Maybe he didn't have the words to talk about it. Maybe I didn't, either.

I checked the clock again. Three minutes since the last time I looked. I needed to stop that; distract myself and the heart-bird banging against my ribs.

Maybe Mam would like it if I drew something, just for her. Maybe she'd be in the mood to look this time. And anyway, drawing helped. Usually.

I got out my new sketchbook – the one I spent two lots of Saturday money on – and the pencil crayons that are just mine and 'too grown-up' for Rio to use. I sharpened them one by one, watched the shavings curl on to the coffee table like apple peel, easy-slow . . .

The door banged open. A Rio explosion in the room. He leaped from sofa to chair like an excited squirrel, two early daffodils from Jo's kitchen jug clutched in his fist. He landed next to me, banged into the table. Crayons skittered and skidded across the floor.

'Take for Mam, Jonah,' he shouted. 'Daff'dils!'

I leaned down, reached for my runaway crayons, began lining them up on the table: greens first, then blues. 'Did Jo say you could have those, Rio?' I asked.

He stopped bouncing, pushed out his chin. His fist tightened around the thin stalks. The flower heads drooped. 'For Mam,' he said.

I nodded. 'But you're supposed to ask first,' I said. 'Did you?'

Rio tightened his grip on the stems. A flower head snapped loose, fell to the floor. He stared down at it. 'Sorry, f'ower,' he whispered. His eyes darted towards the door, round pools of panic. He remembered *that* then: how Mam felt about us breaking things.

He laid the remains of the daffodils on the table next to my paper, wiped sticky strings of sap from his fingers. He threw his arms around my neck. 'Didn't mean to, Jonah,' he whispered. He squeezed on to the chair beside me, curled up like a cat, and started sucking his thumb.

I thought of the first time we took daffodils for Mam. Easter daffodils. Rio cradled them all the way in the car to meet her, even though they made him sneeze. Their yellow faces lit his chin like small suns. The sun was in Mam's eyes when he handed them to her. She smiled. A real smile. But *Rio's* sunshine disappeared when she told us she'd left our Easter eggs on the bus. 'I'll pop them in the post,' she said.

They never arrived.

'It's OK, Rio,' I said. 'Jo won't be cross. She'll understand. She's not – not like Mam.'

Mam who could fizz like an unexpected firework; burn the air with angry words. Mam who didn't care about 'sorry' or 'didn't mean to' . . .

I pointed to the white paper waiting in front of me. 'We could *draw* daffodils, if you like? For Mam . . .'

Rio nodded. 'Jonah do it,' he said. His head pressed against my shoulder, heavy and warm. I let the Easter memory disappear into the green sweep of stalk and leaves, the careful curl of yellow petals and orange trumpet centre. I tried to put the sun there.

Rio stirred, pulled his thumb from his mouth with a pop.

'Happy f'owers, Jonah,' he said. 'So Mam happy too.'

'That's it,' I said, handing him the picture. 'Happy flowers.'

I just hoped we were both right.

We never got to find out.

Mam was waiting for us on Whitby beach. She waved, walked towards us. Slowly, like in one of those black and white movies with no words. Her long hair whipped around her face like seaweed, covered her smile. But it was there. I'm sure it was. She was happy to see us.

The sea was *not*. It threw sand in our eyes, hurled gritty missiles that stung our cheeks. It snatched the daffodil drawing from Rio's hand as he held it out for Mam, spun it off across the sand and sent it tumbling and twisting in the air like an injured bird.

No more happy flowers.

Rio watched it go, still as stone. His face crumpled. Mam looked at me.

'Quick,' she said. She turned and ran towards the sea.

'Last one in's a frog,' she shouted, hands cupped around her mouth like the wind wanted to steal her voice too. She walked out into the waves, still in her socks and shoes.

Rio stared after her, grabbed my hand. 'C'mon, Jonah,' he said. 'Come *on*.'

'OK,' I said, sliding my backpack from my shoulder. But my feet dragged in the sand. Mams weren't supposed to run into the sea. Not on a freezing-cold day. And not in their socks and shoes.

What was going on?

And anyway, that sea did *not* want us here. Mam wasn't listening.

Rio's hand tugged in mine, let go. He hurtled off after Mam.

So no choice. 'Rio, wait,' I called. 'Wait for me.'

But when we tried to paddle, a giant wave snatched his plastic sandal from his foot, whisked it away, making him scream and scream. He tried to walk out into the deepest, darkest, drowning parts to find it. Maybe he was looking for the lost daffodils too, because his Rio-storm was louder and scarier than usual. And Rio was good at storms.

Mam had to carry him back up the beach, promise him hot vinegar chips and new sandals before he stopped kicking her. When his storms came, he forgot to worry about getting told off. He only stopped screaming when we found sunshine-yellow flip-flops in a shop selling rainbow rock. He got two sticks of that too. Even though I said, 'He's not supposed to have too much sugar, and what if he bites off hard, sharp pieces and chokes, because he's only three and a half?'

I don't think Mam heard me over the wind and Rio's whining, because she gave him the rock anyway.

I didn't have any. Chips or rock. One of those whirling

waves was trapped in my stomach, making me feel sick. And it was there before the sea stole Rio's shoe. It was there before Mam turned up, and it got bigger and choppier when she arrived, even though I really wanted to see her.

We sat under the pier while Rio ate his chips. He said they crunched in his teeth. 'That's the sand, that is,' Mam said.

Rio was just about to cry again because he 'didn't want the beach in his tummy' when a fat raindrop splatted him on the nose, made him forget. I got our waterproof jackets out of my rucksack. The wind was in those too, trying to pull them away, puffing them out like blue sails. Rio's face went red when I put his over his head, which meant he was about to lose it again. So I pretended the pier was a massive ship. Its tall legs were the rigging, and we were pirates. Rio loves pirates. Well, he did then.

We searched the wet sand for seashell treasure. Rio tried to persuade a fat seagull to sit on his shoulder like a parrot, but it turned its back on him, flew away. I found him a driftwood telescope instead, and he climbed on the bottom rung of the 'rigging' to look out for enemy ships.

Mam didn't know how to play pirates. I think she felt left out because she went quiet. She kept checking her phone for something, saying, 'We'll have to go soon, mind, boys,' without looking up.

I went and sat with her for a minute because it's not nice being left out. But she just put her phone in her pocket and watched the waves crawl further and further away, like I wasn't even there. Like she was moving further and further away too.

'Pictoors on the sand,' Rio shouted, hopping around like a sea sparrow. 'Draw sand pictoors, Jonah.'

So we found more washed-up sticks and Mam joined in, then. She drew a parrot that looked more like a sausage, and started laughing like maybe she wouldn't be able to stop. Rio laughed too. That was the best bit of the day. Rio's laugh is hiccoughs and happiness rolled up together. When I looked back down the beach, the sea had disappeared; joined up with the sky, like someone had rubbed out the line between. Tiny diamond lights flickered there; a handful of Rio's sticky Christmas glitter. I squeezed my eyes shut, in case the diamonds weren't real, but when I opened them, they were still there.

Mam saw them too. She kept staring and staring like they were calling to her, like she might walk all the way out to sea to find them.

'Mam,' I said, 'Mam . . .?' I touched her sleeve.

She turned, peered at me as if I was hidden in a mist. And then she was back, laughing again, calling to Rio in a pirate voice.

We drew sea dragons and whales, and pirate faces with daft, wonky smiles. I found a smile too, just for a while.

Before we left, Mam wrote our names in the sand:

Jonah

Rio

Marina

She drew a big sand heart around them. 'I love my boys deeper than the sea and forever and ever,' she said. She held our faces between her hands and stared at us for ages, like she was trying to take a photo with her eyes. Her cheeks got all wet, even though it had stopped raining. 'Sea spray,' she said, and she laughed again.

But the tide was a long way out by then, so I knew it wasn't that. And the laugh was thinner this time, different.

Our mam, she can change quicker than blinking. Just like the sea.

On the way back to meet our social worker, Nadia, Mam let us choose something from the gift shop on the pier. 'Just something small, mind, 'cos the Social have messed up my benefits again.'

Rio wanted a cuddly fox that had cloud-soft fur and golden eyes. He clung on to it until his fingers went white and Mam prised them off and shouted at him, because that wasn't 'something small'. And it wasn't. It was something huge for Rio, because foxes are his favourite and he's never had a toy one before. His face went redder than the fox's fur and he was just about to lie down on the shop floor and go crazy when I spotted some bags of marbles tied up with sparkly purple string.

'Pirate *treasure*, Rio,' I said, and his green eyes got round as marbles too.

I got a bag for myself as well, even though I'm a bit old for marbles, because I wanted his smile to stay a bit longer.

It did – it lasted all through tea back at Jo's house; our favourite: tuna and broccoli pasta without any of the crispy bits on top that Rio hates. Jo let us stay up late on her saggy hug of a sofa, made us mugs of cocoa that painted upside-down chocolate smiles on our faces; brought back Rio's hiccough laughter. His chatter bounced around the bathroom like the soap bubbles, while we showered sand from our knees and hair. He giggled when Jo dried between his toes, even though a secret grain of sand still clung there, scratching at his pink skin.

But bubble-bright Rio disappeared when Jo said, 'No flip-flops in bed, sweetheart.' There was another Rio-storm, then. It got into his tummy and threw tuna pasta back out, all over the bedroom carpet and the flip-flops.

'Never mind, Rio,' Jo said. 'How about I rinse the flip-flops, and you can keep them under your pillow for now?'

Rio shook his head, covered his face with his hands and kept sniffling for ages and ages. Then his storm was inside me as well. All the seaside smiles got rinsed away, like they had never even happened. It wasn't Jo's fault. Maybe it was mine.

When Jo went downstairs, I said Rio could put his flip-flops back on again. He fell asleep, then – for a bit.

He had one of his bad dreams, like he always does after we see Mam. I cheered him up with stories about what his old sandal was up to at the bottom of the ocean. How an octopus was wearing it on one of its eight feet, kicking up sea squalls because it didn't have a shoe for the other seven. Or how the sandal had been swallowed by a shark, making him burp humungous sea-bubbles. Rio liked the shark story best. He made me tell it over and over. He knew if any of the words were different. I had to do the bubble-burps too.

'Who tell't you stories when you was little and scared, Jonah?' he asked in his nearly asleep voice.

'Mam did,' I said. She never did, though. I lied. Just like Mam did with her beach words. With her sand heart and the love promise inside it. That's not at the bottom of the ocean with Rio's shoe.

It's nowhere.

It's nothing.

It's wiped away. Disappeared. Swallowed by the greedy waves like it was never there at all. Mam knew that would happen when she drew it.

So did I.

CHAPTER 3
NOW

Mam and the sea, they're sort of the same. You can't trust either of them. But at least the sea keeps coming back up the beach when it's supposed to. Mam, she's best at *not* doing what she's supposed to.

Disappearing is her superpower.

She's missed four contact visits since that Whitby day, which means Rio and I haven't seen her for seven months.

Today it's Rio's fourth birthday. Mam's invited, like always. No one believes she'll come, though. No one except Rio. He's up before the sun, singing 'Happy Birthday' at the top of his voice.

I keep my eyes shut, pretend I'm still asleep. Honestly, I'd like to sleep through the whole day. I can see Rio's colours, blazing bright behind my eyelids. I can't bear to see them get rubbed away by a no-show Mam.

There's no stopping Rio. He lands on my chest like a small missile. He bounces up and down. His fingers are on my eyelids, prising them open. 'Birthday day, Jonah!'

he shouts, peering into my left eye. 'Wake UP!'

I slide from under him. 'Not yet, mate,' I say. 'It's not your birthday till it gets light.'

He wriggles over me, all bony knees and sharp elbows. His feet pitter-patter across the floor.

The flick of a light switch, and yellow explodes behind my eyelids. It's LOUD.

He tugs at my duvet. I give in; open my eyes and pull myself up on my pillows. Rio clambers on top of my feet. 'Presents 'n' cake,' he says, bouncing hard enough to break my ankles. 'And candles and fings.'

'Yep,' I say. 'Brilliant, Rio. Happy birthday!' My mouth takes some persuading, but I grin at him.

Birthdays are good things to Rio. All about glitter and fun and getting things and eating until your belly feels like a balloon about to burst. He's too little to remember the other kind. The empty-tummy empty-house empty-heart kind of birthday.

Mam promised him that day she *would* be here for this one. That day beside the Whitby sea. Rio, he still believes . . .

He's in bouncy Tigger mode all morning, manages to fall off a kitchen chair while helping Jo mix buttercream for his birthday cake. He doesn't even cry.

He stares at the finished dinosaur cake like it's appeared

16

by magic, even though he's watched Jo put it together, fixed its blue Smartie eyes in place all by himself. He keeps counting the candle spines along its back, practising his blowing skills. There are balloons in rainbow colours, streamers, party plates with green and purple dinosaurs smiling from the centre. A 'house' made from tiny sandwich bricks, with a mini-sausage chimney. Curly crisps, yellow jelly with purple and green grapes inside like sunken treasure. Candy-striped biscuits. Everything Rio loves best in the world.

Jo piles presents on the window seat. Even I want to know what's in the bright packages.

Rio doesn't touch a thing.

'Waitin' for Mam,' he says. He grabs a blue velvet cushion from the sofa. 'She likes blue 'cos it's sea colour.' He sets it on a chair at the top of the tea table.

My heart squeezes.

Jo takes him upstairs 'to get ready for his special tea'. When he comes down, he crawls on to the window seat, hands like tiny starfish pressed against the glass.

Jo's had 'that talk' with him again. The one where Mam's not coming today. I can see it in the drop of his shoulders. Some of his colours didn't make it down the stairs. He's still believing, though. That's the worst bit.

I squeeze in next to him, point at the biggest parcel. 'There's an elephant in there,' I say.

Nothing.

I reach for a thin purple package, tied with spotted red ribbon, hold it to my ear.

'Crikey,' I say. 'Someone's bought you a snake. It's a friendly one, though. It's hissing "Happy Birthday". Listen . . .'

But Rio's caught the flash of red outside the window, the crunch of tyres. I peer past him.

Nadia's car. The one that's supposed to have Mam in the passenger seat.

Rio scrambles down, races to the door. 'Mam,' he yells, back in Tigger mode.

'It's Nadia, sweetheart,' Jo says. 'Just Nadia. Like we talked about.'

Nadia bustles in through the door, arms full of presents wrapped in Spider-Man paper. Rio won't even look at them. She hasn't brought the one thing he wanted most.

Mam not turning up, it slices through me like one of Jo's silver cake knives. Even though I knew. Right now, I hate her for cutting pieces out of Rio's heart too. Even though I love her.

Your mam, she's still your mam. Still hooked inside

your ribs somewhere. Even when she's disappeared.

Rio sort of folds in, all empty like a popped balloon, pushes his presents from the window seat and slumps there, knees under his chin. He pushes Nadia away too, turns his back on Jo.

Jo lights the candles on his cake to distract him. Rio, he LOVES candles. Last birthday, he made Jo light them five times over, just so he could blow them out and make more wishes.

He makes *me* blow out the candles this time. He doesn't make a wish.

'Wishes don't work,' he says.

I want to say, 'Of course they do, Rio,' because you should believe in wishes when you're only four, but the words feel like a lie. So instead I tell him maybe Mam lost her phone and didn't get Nadia's calls and texts about the party. And she couldn't ring to pass on a message. I really, *really* want that to be true.

'C'mon, Rio,' I say. 'Have some birthday cake before Nadia eats it all herself. You know what she's like.' I try for another grin, but it sort of slides off my face and the joke falls flat like jelly left out in the sun.

'Mam would want you to have some,' I say. 'It's your favourite, remember?'

Rio shakes his head; folds his arms across his chest. 'Don't want to,' he says. 'An' Nadia can't have none, neither.' He glances up from under his fringe to make sure she hasn't already helped herself. 'Only Jonah can.'

Jo cuts me a huge slice. Jam oozes from it, red as blood. I only eat one bite, because you can't demolish your brother's birthday cake when he's too upset to have any himself.

Rio won't open his presents, either. 'Not till the moon wakes up,' he says. ''Cos Mam might come. She likes helping me do it.' That's when I realise he still believes in wishes.

In the end, he falls asleep on the window seat, draped across the present pile. Jo carries him up to bed and I follow, even though I'm not tired. If he wakes, he'll need one of my stories. I search my head for ideas as we climb the stairs, but the silver knife has cut those away too.

Luckily Rio doesn't even stir when Jo puts him into his pyjamas. Maybe he's pretending this time. Sometimes it's just easier.

Jo and I collect his presents from the dining room, pile them at the foot of his bed for the morning. When she goes downstairs to clear away, I drag the duvet from my room and curl up on the end of his bed, wait for the first nightmare to come, try to find my Rio stories. I'm the only one who knows the ones that work.

Nadia's voice rises in the hall, softens like she just remembered the sleeping Rio.

But I heard it. The 'Otis and I will see you Friday, then. Around four'.

I curl tighter, close against Rio's small legs. Friday. Two days from now.

Why is she coming back so soon?

And who is Otis?

The silver knife is back, jabbing at my heart.

CHAPTER 4

Otis is a man with a shiny bald head and too-shiny shoes, like he polished them up for something important. When he sits down at the kitchen table, I see he's wearing different coloured socks: one brown, one green. Which makes me like him just a little bit. Just for a moment.

He's here because he helps make the best decisions for children, Nadia tells us. I want to say that we can make the best decisions about ourselves. That Shiny-Man doesn't even know me and Rio, so how come he thinks he can decide anything at all? But I don't. Just in case he's not as nice and shiny on the inside and gets annoyed.

I want to ask why he's here, because strangers with briefcases come for Foster Care Review Meetings, and it's not time for one of those. We had one three weeks ago.

'I have to change out of my uniform,' I say, heading for the door.

'OK, Jonah,' Jo says. 'Nadia and Otis and I will have a bit of a chat while you do that. And there'll be a drink and a snack for you when you come down.'

Nadia is smiling as the door snaps shut. Her smile doesn't fit because she's got her serious face on. I stretch my ears to hear what they're saying now that I've left, but Jo's using her quiet-and-important voice and the kettle is singing. Her words can't make it through the noise.

'Play, Jonah.' Rio's voice. 'Play hide-and-seek.' He's there, behind me in the hall, pulling at my sleeve. His eyes are huge and swimmy, because he knows something's up and he doesn't like strangers with briefcases, either. So I say, 'Yes, I'll be seeker!' I start counting to thirty and Rio scampers away, trailing his scraggy yellow comfort blanket behind him. And I'm wishing more than anything in the whole world that we could hide away together and not come out until Mam comes home.

I'm wishing I wasn't too old for a yellow blanket.

Rio won't come out from behind our bedroom curtains, so Jo says she'll stay upstairs with him, read *The Tiger Who Came to Tea* to him, right where he is. Sometimes Jo does know a thing or two about children. And about stories.

I'm not going to like the story that's waiting for me in the kitchen.

Nadia and Shiny-Man are still at the kitchen table. Their elbows are on it, which Mam says is bad manners.

Nadia pulls out the chair next to her and it screams on the tiles. She pulls a face as if that's funny, but it's not and the chair-scream is inside my head too when she starts talking.

'Otis is from the Family Finding Team,' Nadia tells me.

My heart somersaults. 'Is this about Mam?' I say, looking from Otis to Nadia. 'Did you find her?'

Nadia's hand slides over mine. 'No, Jonah. I'm sorry. We've still not heard from your mam.'

Then it's like they're a double act, her and Otis. Rambling on about it being time to get me and Rio more settled, about looking to the future. About Mam not being able to care for us.

Otis keeps blinking and nodding like a clockwork owl whenever Nadia is speaking. Nadia does the same whenever it's his turn to talk. I think they worked out their words together beforehand, like a play script, because they don't feel real. They don't like them all that much, either, even though they soft-serious-smile as if they do. Otis's foot tap-taps under the table, like mine does when I'm worried, and Nadia keeps twisting her silver thumb-rings round and round and round. Little sparks of light jump from them, like when you rub two sticks together to start a fire in dry grass and twigs. Only the fire's in me. In my face. In my chest. Burning. Getting bigger and bigger.

Nadia lays her hand on mine. I snatch it away. Turn my head.

'I know this is very hard, Jonah,' she says. 'But your mam, she's nowhere to be found. We've tried very hard to find her, we really have. But you and Rio, you need to be settled now.'

The flames roar in my ears. I put my hands over them.

Jo's here now, sitting next to me. 'I think maybe Jonah needs a few minutes,' she says. 'How about we go in the garden for a bit of air, sweetheart?'

I shake my head. I slam my hands down on the table. 'NO. Mam WILL come back. You don't know her. She WILL.'

Nadia waits. There's only the roar of the fire and the tapping of Otis's foot. I feel Jo's eyes on me, feel the pain in them, like this is burning her too. I can't look at her.

Otis is speaking now, and it's like he's speaking in capital letters. Underlining them as he goes. It's decided. They <u>DON'T BELIEVE MAM'S COMING BACK FOR ME AND RIO THIS TIME</u>. Or if she does, it might not be for a long time. <u>TOO LONG</u>. And she's <u>NOT RELIABLE</u> when she <u>IS</u> around. We need <u>PROPER CARE</u>. They're asking a judge to make an order that says Social Services can find us a <u>FOREVER FAMILY</u>. <u>SO YOU CAN SETTLE</u>. <u>KNOW WHERE YOU ARE</u>.

Words fly out, tearing through my throat, tearing the air:

Me and Rio and Mam, we ARE forever family,

and no one can say we're not.

Mam will change her mind – she'll come back.

She will . . .

Nobody's listening. Or if they are, they don't want to hear. They've already decided. <u>HAD MEETINGS</u>. <u>BEEN TO COURT</u>. Without me and Rio even being there.

They're putting our photos on a website for kids that need families, they say. Nadia, Otis and Jo will agree some words about us to go underneath, like a kind of advert. I can help with the words. We can write things like how Rio loves animals and pirates and marbles, how his smile and his imagination are as big as the sky, and how he needs stories and reassurance at night. I tell them to write that Rio needs *me* at night, that he needs *my* stories and *my* drawings and that *I'm* better than anyone at those things. Those are the special things about me. I can't think of any others.

I want to say don't write that I'm Bad-Luck Jonah. Don't write about my *worries* that explode sometimes. But I'm too scared to say the words out loud and make them real.

It won't make any difference anyway. Everyone will want Rio, even though his bright colours are hiding in the pictures. But who would want me: a nearly eleven-year-old, with no colours except blood-red angry or ash-grey sad-and-worried? A boy that brings bad luck wherever he goes. No one. I already know that.

'You know, Jonah, it's the law that Social Services must try to keep brothers and sisters together,' Nadia says. 'Well, we have to do our very best anyway. If it's the <u>RIGHT THING</u> for both of them, that is . . .'

Which means it's not really 'the law' at all.

'We're going to do our very best for you and Rio, Jonah,' Otis says. 'And if that means keeping you together, then we'll try to make it happen, I promise.' He takes off his glasses, lays them down on the table.

I think he means the promise, even though he's stopped speaking in capitals letters, because his eyes look straight into mine; still, like small lakes when there's no wind. Not like Mam's eyes that shift from side to side all the time and hide things, like the sea.

But promises, they get washed away. Like Rio's sandal and Mam's sand heart.

Sunk, without a trace.

Nadia is talking again. I'm miles away, somewhere, watching her mouth move. She stops. She's waiting for me to say something, but I'm falling, dissolving into the watery whooshing sound inside me.

Words float above my head: they don't fit together. They don't make any sense. My breath is stop-start gulps but there's no air.

I'm drowning.

So's Rio, and I'm supposed to save him, but I don't know how.

My hands claw at nothing and then there are plates and cups flying, and splinters of china; tiny arrows in the air around me.

The floor scrapes and scratches beneath my shoes. Jo's arms are tight around me like a lifebelt. Or a trap.

Rio's face is framed in the doorway, pale as plaster. And I've just shown Nadia and Otis that they should get me as far away from him as possible.

CHAPTER 5
ONE MONTH LATER

I was right.

Grown-up promises. They're just like wishes. They never work. Not for long anyway.

Not even my own.

Why would they? I'm Bad-Luck Jonah.

'It's my lovely mum –' Jo tells us – 'she's had a fall and broken some bones – had to go into hospital.'

'Sorry,' I say. And I am. Even though a mam with a few bits broken is still better than one that's disappeared altogether.

'Can they mend her?' Rio asks. He jumps down from the back of the sofa, comes to stand (on one leg) by Jo's chair.

Jo nods. 'Yes, they can, Rio, but she's an old lady so she's going to need a lot of help when she gets out of hospital.' Her brow wrinkles. 'She can't live on her own any more, so . . .'

'Are we going to live at her house?' Rio tips his head on

one side. 'Has she got a pond with goldfish in it? Or a swing?'

Jo smiles. 'No, sweetheart. She hasn't. But maybe *you* will have one day, eh?'

Rio's brow is a puzzle. He runs to look out of the window at Jo's handkerchief garden. He doesn't understand that this isn't a 'forever garden'. How could he?

'The thing is, Jonah,' Jo goes on. 'My mum – she'll be coming to live here.'

'That's OK,' I say.

But it's not. Not for me and Rio. I can feel it.

'Thank you, Jonah,' Jo says. Her hands fall in her lap. She twists them together. 'But you see, Mum's going to need a lot of attention. A lot of my time. Hospital visits, then her care when she gets here.'

'I'll help,' I say. 'I'm good at helping. I helped our mam loads: washing and making beans on toast, brushing Rio's hair, getting shopping. Loads of things . . .'

Jo nods. 'I know. And it's good to be helpful. You're a kind boy. But those things are not your job. They're mine. They're for adults to be doing.' She lifts a strand of hair from my eyes. 'Thing is, I'm not going to be able to look after you and Rio the way you deserve – not going to be able to give you my proper attention, not with Mum to care for . . .'

My heart is battering my ribs, like it's trying to get out. What's happening here?

'And Mum will have to have your bedroom, Jonah . . .'

I start to say that's OK because I always end up in Rio's bed anyway, telling him stories, chasing away the bad dreams.

Jo shakes her head. 'I'm sorry, Jonah, love. I've spoken to Nadia – suggested we try it for a bit. Because, sweetheart, I'd love you both to stay. As long as possible. But there's a rule: each foster child has to have a room of their own, you see.'

'What, then?' I say. 'Me and Rio have to move out?'

Jo shifts in her chair. Like people do when bad news is coming. Even worse news.

'Nadia thinks Rio should stay here,' she says. There's a crack in her voice. She clears her throat. 'With him being the youngest. And you know, Jonah, she thinks it might be good for you to be somewhere where you have all the attention, where you can be "Just Jonah", lovely Jonah, and not have to worry about Rio all the time.' She looks right into my eyes. 'Because I know you do, don't you?'

I stare back at her, a wild, angry sea whooshing in my head.

Rio and me. We're being split up. Just like that.

This can't be happening. Not because an old lady fell down.

Not because of some stupid rule about rooms.

I push down the storm inside me. If I let it out again, I'll be proving Nadia right to move me.

I take a deep breath. It judders and jerks in my chest. 'Whoever made up that stupid rule,' I say – softly, so Rio can't hear – 'they don't know how it feels when your mam vanishes and all you've got left of your life is your brother. If they did, they wouldn't make him disappear too.'

I glance at Rio, happily drawing stick men on the misted windowpane.

'I bet they don't know how nightmares feel, either,' I whisper.

The wild sea starts to escape down my cheeks. I swipe the tears away before Rio notices.

I *promised* him he'd always have me, and I'd always have him. But the social workers are making me a liar already, just like Mam.

I need a plan. And fast. Because me and Rio, we're stitched together like threads in a jumper. If they pull us apart, we'll both unravel, and we won't be Rio or Jonah any more. We won't be anything.

CHAPTER 6

It's happening.

I'm moving to live with this 'long-term' foster carer called Mimi, in a bay that's got something to do with Robin Hood (who isn't even real). It's one hour and six minutes in the car from Rio and Jo. I timed it when Nadia took me for 'an introduction' at Mimi's stupid small house. There was tea and tuna sandwiches, with crisps and tomatoes on the side, and a one-eyed black cat that kept jumping on the table and staring with a mean, yellow, 'you're not wanted here' eye.

Apparently, the 'introduction' went well, even though I said I hate tuna and cats (not true) and I like living in a town not at the seaside (true). And that 'no way am I moving anywhere without Rio'. And even though I didn't look at Mimi the whole time I was there.

Two days from now – Saturday – I am moving. There. *This* Saturday.

Without my brother.

Nadia's explained it all lots of times. So has Jo. It still doesn't make sense.

I'm still drowning.

Everyone is still lying.

I'm not moving because of Jo's mam. That's not true. She's been living with us for two weeks now. She doesn't even take up much space. She's thin like paper and twigs. Her skin's pale and covered in spiderweb cracks, like the plaster walls in our old flat with Mam. Like it might fall away if she moved too much. She mainly just dozes in the big chair in the lounge, and I think she'd sleep there at night if Jo let her because she climbs stairs one step at a time. Like Rio did when he was smaller. It takes her ages. If she slept downstairs, she wouldn't get so worn out, and I could keep my room.

She doesn't take up much of Jo's time, either. She just mooches about in the conservatory, bent on her stick over Jo's pots of bright red flowers. For ages, so Rio thinks she's got stuck. She doesn't even seem sick any more so I reckon she could go home. Her eyes are bird-bright-blue behind her glasses. They're the only bit of her that hasn't got old. Anytime I'm near her, she looks right into the middle of me – right into the big black empty hole where I'm supposed to be Rio's brother, right into my hiding place.

Like she's the only one that can *see* me.

I'm not moving because of her. I'm moving because I'm a rubbish big brother and Nadia thinks my messed-up, bad-luck bits are rubbing off on Rio. She's not saying. But I *know*.

I'm moving because I got angry and shouted and smashed Jo's plates.

Because I'm Bad-Luck Jonah and bad luck follows me around.

Jo says none of that's true, either. But it is. Just look at my life so far.

The clocks tick faster than usual all through Thursday and Friday, but my legs and arms are heavy and slow, filled with stones.

Rio keeps saying, 'When's Saturday?' every five minutes, and rubbing circles on the wet windows so he can check for Nadia's danger-red car. Which doesn't help. My stomach has wild waves in it the whole time, so I haven't eaten a thing for two days. I hear Jo on the telephone to Nadia telling her I'm 'struggling a bit', and that's when I do a bed-door-barricade thing in my room, because she's *wrong* and she's supposed to know about children. I'm much more than struggling a bit; I'm breaking apart. I'm an old boat in a storm. Soon I'll sink without a trace, or just be splinters of myself, drifting and lost, and no one will be able to put me together again.

I pray and pray that Nadia's car won't start on Saturday morning. Or that Mam will come back and put a stop to all this.

The praying doesn't work. Nor does the bed-barricade. I didn't really think they would.

Jo's packed all my things in two blue suitcases, with my photos of Mam and Rio on the top inside the biggest one. Nadia's going to make me a new Life Story book, she says, so that's not in there.

'She should make me a new life,' I say. I drag the coat she bought me out of the case, hurl it on the floor. 'I'm taking my old one,' I say. 'The one Mam bought me.'

The sleeves are too short and there are holes in the pockets, but Jo doesn't say that. She shows me where it's carefully folded in the case with the photos, and her mouth goes tight like mine does when I'm trying not to cry.

I give Rio my bag of marbles and my favourite fossil to keep for me, so he knows we'll see each other again.

'Double t'easure,' he says. But he doesn't smile. He just

says he wants to come and live near Robin Hood as well, because Robin Hood is brave and he'll look after us. I should tell him that Robin Hood isn't there, but his chin is wobbling like the yellow jelly Jo made for his birthday tea, so I don't.

Jo picks Rio up – which he usually hates. But he doesn't struggle. He's floppy, like he's lost all his stuffing and he buries his face in her shoulder.

Jo strokes his hair. 'We'll see Jonah soon, for a visit,' she says.

Rio doesn't move because that sounds like a grown-up promise, and he already knows about those. And because 'visits' are things that don't always happen, just like with Mam.

When Jo puts him down, I whisper in his ear that we'll be together properly soon. I hook his tiny finger. 'Jonah-pinkie-promise,' I say. 'I've got a plan.'

I don't, but I'm going to find one. Because big-brother pinkie-promises are different. Unbreakable. They have to be.

Rio doesn't cry when I get in the car without him. Not this time. He's learning to keep the screams and tears inside, just like me. I don't think that's a good lesson. Not really. They hurt more, trapped in there. And sometimes they sort of explode and make your body do things you don't really mean, things that upset people. Things that don't help at all. Things that hurt *you* the most.

Like this morning, when I ripped all the photos of Mam out of my stupid Life Story book, made a snowstorm with pieces of us fluttering to the carpet like broken birds.

I wish I hadn't.

What if I forget her face?

CHAPTER 7

It's three weeks since they made me leave my brother behind. Three weeks, two days, six hours and twenty-three minutes, to be exact, since our social worker made me come and live here with Mimi, in her stupid ancient cottage, with stupid sloping walls and spiders the size of small cats. In a sloping street that looks like it's sliding down towards the sea. In fact, everything in this town looks like it's doing the same.

A 'long-term placement'. That's what they called it. Which makes me sound like an object and not a person. But there's no chance of me staying 'permanently' anywhere that doesn't have Rio in it. And Mimi's house doesn't look like it's going to last much longer in any case.

I've been staying in my room as much as I can get away with. Except for mealtimes, because Mimi insists, and when Nadia made me visit the school I'm supposed to start after Easter – soon as there's a place. (It smells of potatoes and disinfectant and there are miles of corridors like tunnels, with floors that squeak under your shoes, so everyone looks at you. No chance I'll be going there again.)

My room's got a sloping ceiling, like the rest of Mimi's house, and wonky narrow windows. There are thick wooden beams on the overhead, so low near the door that they steal strands of my hair if I don't remember to duck. There's a curved one above the staircase that makes it look like you're climbing up inside a tunnel.

The walls by my bed leave dusty marks on my clothes when I brush against them, like they're crumbling away bit by bit, might fall down any second. That's probably to do with the sea, because it hisses a warning at me through the gap around the old window frames and fills the room with its salty stink if you open the window even a crack. But it's still better up here in my room – better *anywhere* indoors – than outside. *Everywhere* outside in Robin Hood's Bay is *far* too near the sea . . .

But I've made good use of all that alone time. I've made a book. For Rio. It's full of stories I've made up, and there are drawings on every page to help him understand what's happening to the characters. The octopus is there, still wearing a yellow sandal, and in that one, he's an octopus king, and Rio is an intrepid deep-sea diver, hunting for sunken treasure to exchange for the sandal – which is made of pure gold.

Nadia's collecting it to give to Rio. It's full of Jonah. So Rio will know I haven't forgotten him.

It's also part of my plan.

All that time in my room, it helped me to see. It's simple.

If Nadia and Shiny-Man think I'm a bad influence on Rio – bad luck to be around – I just need to show them that they're wrong. Keep my worried bits, my red-scribble angry bits and my bad luck to myself and be the BEST Jonah I can be. The BEST big brother anyone could have. Ever.

Writing books for Rio, that's part one of the plan.

Part two is being as helpful and cooperative as possible with Mimi.

Part three – and this is the toughest part – is not worrying about the sea. (Pretending will probably have to do. That's going to be hard enough.)

So today I've agreed to go out with Mimi after lunch 'for a bit of fresh air and a look at the town'. Not that we need to go out for fresh air. There's already loads of it sneaking in through the windows and walls, just like it did in our last flat with Mam. Only, to be fair, *that* air smelled of the bins outside Bill's Cafe underneath us, and here it only smells a bit salty.

'That'll be lovely, Jonah,' Mimi says. 'I've a few groceries to buy while we're out, but it's treat time, too. You decide: the biggest cake you can find in George's Bakery, or an ice cream down by the seafront.' She peers out of the window at the pencil-grey clouds that have hung there all morning. 'Not the best day for the beach,' she says. 'But you can get your first look at the bay, if you like. Beautiful, it is. Beautiful.'

No. Not the bay. Not yet.

'I hate ice cream,' I say. Which isn't true. I love it. Especially mint choc chip. And the sort with strawberry sauce rippled through it like marble. Sometimes words just come out without me knowing they're going to.

Jonah the Best Big Brother would say, 'Yes, please!' He'd make a really big thing about how kind Mimi was to offer. I need to do better. Be much better. Much braver.

'It's just, I mean, thank you, Mimi,' I say. 'Only, it's still a bit cold for ice cream.' My voice shrinks mouse-small, not brave at all. 'But I'd love to see the bay another day.'

Mimi smiles. 'Whatever you want, pet. Pop your coat and hat on, then. There'll be a wind off the sea in town today. And you're right. It's chilly, even for March.'

There's a wind off the sea in the front room too, lifting

the edges of the curtains, just because it can. I think about saying that. I don't. And Mimi doesn't say anything when I fetch my skinny old coat instead of the new one with shiny buttons and thick fur inside.

I keep my head down as we walk, in case I get a glimpse of the sea down below the town and my legs won't work. I don't want Mimi getting suspicious right away. Some of the streets slope so much that my feet go faster and faster, even though I don't tell them to. Goodness knows how the clusters of pink, white and grey cottages manage to cling on there. There's climbing ivy and other green stuff crawling all over their walls. Maybe that's what's holding them up, rooting them to the ground.

The fishy-salty sea smell gets stronger and stronger. There are slip-slide-twist-your-ankle cobbles everywhere. And now they are shiny-wet. If Mimi makes us walk any faster, we'll hurtle helter-skelter straight down on to the beach. The tide will be right in. Probably a freak tide, higher than it's ever been. Deep and dark and dangerous.

Because this is still me. Bad-Luck Jonah. And that's just the way things go.

Being brave is hard.

Mimi smiles. 'Nearly there,' she says. 'George's is two minutes from the beach,' she adds. As if that's a good thing.

She waves to a woman pushing a baby in a buggy and a tall, stringy boy going much too fast on a red scooter. She chats on, points out narrow shops with striped beach balls, buckets, spades and fishing nets swaying from hooks, metal ice-cream signs groaning in the wind. She stops at the bottom of a stone staircase rising between two old buildings. A green wooden arrow points up the steps, which are squeezed inside the narrow alleyway. They're wonky, worn thin in places like thousands of pairs of feet have climbed them.

'Great little museum at the top,' Mimi announces. 'Specially if you're interested in fossils and shipwrecks and the like, which I'll bet you are.' She searches my face for a flicker of interest.

I *do* like fossils. I like how you can just look at them and know all about the living things imprinted there: when they lived, what they ate for dinner, even. Which family they belonged to, and what they all looked like. Which is more that you can say for me and Rio. Or Mam, who doesn't even know who her birth mam and dad were. And that means there's a big full stop around who me and Rio are, too. And we've never even seen a photo of our dads.

Fossils, they make me feel sort of safe and still and part of something.

Shipwrecks, though. I don't even want to *think* about those.

I don't say any of this to Mimi. I wouldn't know where the words live. Besides, the less she knows about me, the better. I try for a 'Best Big Brother' smile instead.

Mimi leans in closer, lowers her voice like she's sharing a secret. 'This old town has some exciting history, you know, Jonah. We had smugglers in the bay not so many years back. Pirates too, back in the day. So they say.' She laughs, shakes her head. I feel the smile drop from my face like the wind took it without asking. And I'm there again: Whitby beach. With stick-picture pirates in the sand, Rio's bright-bubble laugh, and a promise about to be washed away with the tide.

A seagull screams overhead. I pull my hat right down over my ears. I stumble half-blind around the next corner and bump into Mimi. She's stopped outside a shop window that's curved like the bow of a ship. She ferrets around in her enormous shopping bag, pulls out her purse, presses two pound coins into my hand. 'What d'you fancy, then? Got a favourite, have you?' She nods towards the baker's window, where rows of golden pies and sausage rolls line up with bulging cream slices, cherry-topped buns and gooey chocolate somethings that I've never seen before.

I shake my head because I feel sick and I'm about to say, 'take me back', when a fox appears – out of nowhere.

She's all sand-caked, stringy fur and eyes like searchlights. Wild, wary eyes. Eyes like the ones I see in the mirror when I'm alone. Like the wild worry in me made real, there on the pavement. She stops dead, stands there, on the other side of the street, staring at me with one ear up and one ear down, as if she's trying to work out who I am. Whether she should run . . .

She looks thin. Thinner than the foxes that lurked behind walls and circled the bins back when we lived with Mam. You could smell them, feel their quick eyes on you, hear their quick feet in the alleyways as they made off with half-eaten burgers, the leftovers from the takeaways on every corner.

This fox looks hungry.

Hungry hurts.

'I like those,' I say, pointing at the biggest of the flaky sausage rolls in George's window. Mimi raises one eyebrow. And this time, she's got X-ray vision like Jo's mam.

'Best not encourage foxes, pet,' she whispers. 'Shopkeepers don't like them hanging around. Nor do their customers. Best she scarpers before someone calls Pest Control. They keep a close watch between now and

Easter – that's when the holidaymakers start arriving, with their chip papers and ice-cream wrappers and half-eaten burgers everywhere. Foxes are a real problem if they're still about then; hanging around the beach, upsetting people. Shame, but there it is.'

But she looks the other way when we leave the shop, pretends not to see when I take one bite of my warm sausage roll then drop the bag with the rest of it on the pavement. Maybe she knows what she said is not fair. Which it definitely isn't. Because I bet the foxes were here first, before this stupid wonky town with its bricks and cement and cobbles. I bet there were forests to hide in and fresh-caught food in their fox-bellies, instead of fast-food leftovers and people moving them on so there's nowhere to call home any more.

I look back over my shoulder as we walk away, watch the fox gobble my food-gift down in two mouthfuls, butter-soaked bag and all. She stares up at me again and something passes between us. She's saying thank you. I know she is. She licks her lips with a long pink tongue, keeps on staring. It's hard to look away.

The shop doorbell clangs. The fox dashes down an alleyway at the side, just as 'Probably George' emerges red-faced and folds his arms over his round stomach.

He shakes his head, turns, and plods back into his shop.

Mimi hands me a paper bag – a second sausage roll inside it. Heat seeps from it, warms my cold fingers. I hope the fox feels a bit warmer now too.

'Don't go worrying yourself about that fox, now, Jonah,' Mimi says as we reach a gift shop with glittering necklaces and rings in the window. 'Wild things, they know how to survive. And she looked like a young 'un to me. Like as not she's got family close by to look out for her. She'll not be on her own. But she needs to learn to keep away from the town.'

I wait outside a tiny Spar round the corner, watch Mimi squeeze between narrow aisles with tall stacks of tins and packets. Even those are wonky.

She keeps looking back at me while she fills her basket, like she thinks I might make a run for it too. Which I might if I had anywhere else to go. Grease soaks through the bag in my hand. I stare at the dark patches blooming on the paper and hope my sausage roll isn't the only thing the young fox has to eat today. And that her family haven't left her all alone. Because families: they're not always where they're supposed to be.

My fist tightens around the remains of my sausage roll. Crushes it flat.

I keep watch for the fox as we climb back through the streets, Mimi's bulging bag clinking between us. No sign. Nothing. I remember about being the Best Big Brother and offer to carry the bag. It's super heavy. I sling it over my shoulder and try to look like it's nothing. By the time we get to Mimi's street, my arm feels like it might fall off. Before we go indoors, I check again for the fox, but I can't even see to the end of the road. The sea has thrown a mist over us, over everything. Just like that.

'Gets right into your bones, this sea mist,' Mimi says. 'Comes out of nowhere too.' She reaches towards my collar, like she might be going to turn it up for me. Like I do for Rio.

Did for Rio.

I jerk my head away from Mimi's hand, then wish I hadn't. She stuffs it inside her pocket. 'Should be seeing signs of spring weather by now,' she says, her voice muffled as she tucks her chin down inside her coat. 'But the North Sea has its own ideas. That's just the way of things.'

I shoot her a glance. Why did she say that? Does she know I'm scared?

Once we're indoors, she makes me hot chocolate and I drink it, even though my stomach's still churning like the sea. 'Best chocolate ever,' I say, even though it tastes the same as Jo's.

A fire jumps red and gold in the lounge because Mimi, she 'feels the cold these days. Thin old bones,' she says. 'Out there in a T-shirt in all weathers, I was, when I were a girl.' She shivers. Laughs.

Rio, he hates the cold even though his bones are new. His 'cold' comes from the black hole in the middle of him. The one Mam made when she kept leaving us on our own. My throat squeezes. I hope he's warm today. I hope Jo remembers he needs a T-shirt under his jumpers and sweatshirts, or he goes ballistic about them tickling his skin. I hope that if he gets a new forever family, they know not to buy him things that fit tight: like he's 'being squashed'.

I hope he doesn't get a new family before I can rescue him and put our real family back together again. I can't let that happen.

My chest tightens like *I'm* being squashed right now, and I feel smaller, smaller, smaller. Nothing, nothing, nothing like the new, brave Good-Luck Jonah I need to find.

I'll try harder tomorrow.

CHAPTER 8

The mist hangs outside my bedroom window that night: curls and twists of it; pale ghosts in the weak moonlight, trying to get into the warm. I turn away, pin my duvet around me, super tight. I'm one of the secret summer caterpillars in their cocoons, clinging to the scratchy grass on the rec near my old school. Hiding away until I can grow my wings and fly in search of bright flowers. And freedom.

I worry about Rio. Did Jo tell him his bedtime story tonight?

Has a new family chosen him yet?

Has Nadia given him the book I made? I need him to know I haven't abandoned him like Mam.

I don't sleep for ages, and when I do, I dream of the skinny young fox, her empty stomach pressing her on through endless, shrouded, sliding streets. She looks back over her shoulder, keeps stopping as if waiting for someone. Now she's Rio in a pirate hat, stretching out his hand towards me. Then, suddenly, no more streets. Just the sea, rearing high like a great black horse, curling around him, carrying him away. And rainbow colours dissolving in the darkness.

I wake with an ache in my stomach, my throat scratchy and dry. As I reach for my cup of water, yellow searchlight eyes stare at me through the misty window glass. I blink a couple of times. Creep across the carpet, stand on tiptoe by the window, my warm breath clouding the cold panes.

There's nothing to see but the slide of the moon and the shadowy slope of rooftops in the velvet-black night.

When I ease back my bedroom curtains in the morning, the sun's out, painting pink and yellow streaks over the rooftops. The wind's dropped, because I don't get goosebumps under my pyjama sleeves as I kneel on the bed, peering out. No hiss and smell of the sea. A quiet day. Maybe that means the tide is out. I hope it's out in Whitby as well, because this afternoon we have to go back there.

I'm seeing Nadia. I'm supposed to tell her how I'm feeling, how I'm settling in. Talk through my worries. Which I can't, because they're too big to fit in my mouth, too sharp to make into words. And anyway, how does she expect me to feel now that she's stolen my brother and made me live with strangers? If she can't work that one out, she shouldn't even be a social worker. Besides, it's because of 'my worries' that we've ended up in this situation in the first place. I know it is. So I'm not likely to admit to any more and make things worse.

'Thought we might take lunch down on the beach today, Jonah,' Mimi says over breakfast. 'On the way to see Nadia?' I pretend not to have heard, crunch harder on my cereal. 'It's the best day we've had for ages. Might even find the odd fossil after the late storms we've been having. Like as not there'll be one or two washed down from the cliffs.'

I look up, my mouth full of cornflakes I can't swallow. Stormy seas. I've heard about those.

Mimi is still talking, leaning in towards me like she has another of her secrets to share. 'Best time to find fossils, after a storm,' she says. 'Specially if there's been a rockfall. A high sea washes them from the cliff face. The north side of the bay's the place people find the best ones, in winter. Mighty dangerous round there, though, at that time of year.' I feel sick. A sea powerful enough to steal fossils from stone . . .

I bet it could reach Mimi's street, if it got angry

enough . . . wash it clean away.

I drop my spoon into my bowl. 'There won't be any more, though, will there?' I say. 'Storms? Not when it's nearly spring?'

Mimi laughs. 'Oh, quite possibly, Jonah, love. The North Yorkshire coast's got a mind of its own. But don't you worry – we'll find you some fossils, storm or no storm. On sale everywhere in the town, they are.'

My heart beats danger in my ears so I can't hear anything, but Mimi's mouth has stopped moving so she must be waiting for me to say something. She *mustn't* see Jonah the Coward. Time for Jonah the Best Big Brother.

'Great,' I say. 'Rio loves fossils. Maybe I could ring him up when we get back, tell him about them.' I pick up my spoon, twist it in my hands so they don't start shaking. My face looks back at me all pulled out of shape, like in the Hall of Mirrors on the pier where Rio screamed because his head looked like a banana and he wanted his old one back.

Mimi tips more cereal into my bowl, moves the milk jug towards me. Her eyes are soft at the corners. 'Next week, Jonah, love,' she says. 'Remember? Nadia said you can call Rio next week.'

The red-scribble feelings are in my head now, crawling

down into my arms and legs. Because me and Rio, we're locked up with rules that are like bars, and we haven't even done anything wrong. Locked up near a sea that gets angry when you're not expecting it. Just like Mam.

I'm a storming sea. My foot kicks the table leg and I didn't even know it was going to do that. Milk jumps, splash-slops over the side of the bowl. My spoon flies in the air, clatters on to the table like a silver scream.

I put my hands over my ears, because you don't kick and you don't make a mess and you don't waste food, and Mimi's voice will be thunder-loud, like Mam's on a storm day.

And because I can't even be the Best Big Brother past breakfast time.

But there's only quiet. And Mimi's hand curling over mine like a feather.

CHAPTER 9

We drive to the seafront in Mimi's car, which is bright blue and shaped like three bubbles stuck together. I have to sit in the front, with only the thin, wide windscreen between me and the winding, wonky streets that lead to the sea. It feels even more like we're going to hurtle into it than it did when we were walking.

The higgledy-piggledy cluster of shops and winding alleyways come to a sudden stop. Like the town skidded to a halt just as it reached the beach. Mimi thrusts her foot forward and the bubble car does the same. We're in a tiny car park, where two upside-down boats are fastened to the wall with thick ropes – so that the sea can't snatch them. I scan the horizon. No sign of the sea coming for them – or us – at the moment. Mimi parks up and says, 'You jump out, Jonah, if you like. Have a little look at the beach there. I've a phone call to make, then I'll join you with our picnic. OK?'

I want to wait for her, but I jump out, look around.

A last few buildings sit high above the car park, huddled together like they're scared as well. Looped fishing nets, coiled ropes – and a lifebelt – hang from the side of a grey building: no windows, and sort of twisted away from the sea. Netted cages – lobster pots, I think – are stacked on one side. They're roped down too . . .

You go down a steep stone slipway to the beach. It's got a brick wall and handrails to hang on to along one side. People are leaning there, looking down: a man with a skinny white dog, a woman in a massive hat. A mam with a toddler in a buggy. I stay at the top. By the lifebelt. Which looks like it's had a lot of use.

The slipway is shiny, wet, as if the sea climbed it earlier. Or tossed great waves over the wall just because it could.

I'm not walking on it.

I shield my eyes with my hand and stand on tiptoe. The beach stretches for what looks like miles: pale sand, spread with flat, dark islands that might be seaweed or other cast-offs of the sea. Long, glittering pools of water lie between them.

Tide not completely out, then.

The sea is a flat metal strip, lurking on the horizon.

Two seagulls swoop overhead, wings spread wide. They collide at the bottom of the slipway, scream at one another over a bundle of paper there. I watch their mini tug of war, follow the winner as he takes off, circles away with something dangling from his hooky beak. The loser hops up on to the handrail, puffs out his feathers and shakes them out in a kind of 'seagull shrug' that says he doesn't care. He does, though. He does.

I turn away, look out towards the sea again. She's there.

The fox. *My* fox. Balanced on a rock, staring out along the sand, still as stone. Like she's part of it all: carved into the ancient rock like the fossils. Like there's no one else here but her. Her red and white coat is like a flag against the sky. I edge a few steps towards her, hands tight on the handrail. Even from here, I can tell she's dripping wet. Like *she* might have come from the sea too, just like Mam.

The child in the buggy shouts. The fox turns, shakes a thousand sea-crystals into the air and looks my way. Our eyes lock again. She's trying to say something. I'm sure she is.

She jumps down, scoots along the beach with a scuffle of sand, a whip of white-tipped tail, and disappears around a curve of tall grey cliffs. Just for a moment, I want to follow her. Maybe that's what she wanted me to do . . .

Mimi's struggling towards me with the biggest picnic basket I've ever seen. Not that I've seen any, except on the telly. She points to a bench near the top of the slipway and heaves the basket into the middle of it. 'Still a bit damp and cold to sit on the sand,' she says. I nod and tell her I don't like sand in my sandwiches anyway, just in case lunch by the sea is a thing round here.

She offers me fat tuna sandwiches from a tightly packed plastic box, and this time I do start eating one in case I've already annoyed her too much with my spoon and milk throwing. The fish still smells of the sea, even with mayonnaise plastered all over it, and I wonder how long it is since it was swimming free there, what it felt like to be pulled from its home on a hook. Then I feel sorry for it and can't eat any more.

Mimi puts hers down too. 'Want to talk about it, Jonah?' she asks. 'Best get things out in words before they burst out through those arms and legs of yours.' I stare down at my half-eaten sandwich, feeling as trapped as the used-to-be fish, search for something safe to say.

'That fox was here,' I say. 'On the beach.' I point off to the left. 'She went that way . . . just sort of, disappeared.'

Mimi nods, puts the lid back on her plastic sandwich box. 'She probably hides out in one of the caves. I bet she knows her way around the tunnels too. That'll be how she popped up in town the way she did the other day . . .'

She pauses, reaches for a flask, pours hot chocolate into a blue mug and hands it to me. She pours herself tea from another flask, which says KEEP SMILIN' on the side.

'Tunnels?' I say intrigued, even though I don't know what to do with my dead-fish sandwich and not being allowed to ring Rio is making my insides feel dead too. Because people in films escape through tunnels – even wartime soldiers locked up behind barbed wire and with guards everywhere. And, well, you never know. I might need a Plan B.

I watch Mimi over the rim of the mug because that way I'm half-hidden. Chocolate-scented steam warms my cheeks and when I take a drink it's actually better than Jo's hot chocolate this time, and I never thought that was possible.

Mimi blows on her tea and settles back in her seat. She nods. 'Tunnels, yes. Smugglers' tunnels. A proper network of them there are, Jonah, leading from caves deep into the cliff and then out into the town – into the cellars of some of the oldest houses, the pubs too – through hidden trapdoors and cupboards.' She shakes her head. 'You likely think this is a boring, sleepy little place, after living in the city, but back in the day – specially in the seventeen and eighteen hundreds – smugglers ran riot here, they did.'

Her eyes grow wide just like Rio's when he listens to my stories. Like she's seeing it all happening right now. 'They sailed into the bay, ships loaded down with illegal goods: gin, whisky, tea, silk. And sometimes guns: muskets and all, to hide and sell on. The lucky ones – those whose ships didn't get wrecked on the cliff, or capsized rowing to shore in their little boats – they made a good living. Left with bags of money. Mind you, a fair few got caught by the coastguard as they ran up the beach or, well, less said about what happened to them, the better.'

I see it too. Men with creased faces, furiously rowing against giant waves as the sea fights to drag them under, stolen goods and all. I see greedy eyes and mean mouths filling with water, and I wonder how being captured by the coastguard could ever be worse than being taken by the sea. I see the 'lucky' few, picture their desperate crawl through dark, dripping tunnels, burrowing deeper and deeper into the cliff face, with the sea chasing at their heels, hissing in their ears. I shudder. Why would anyone do that? Suddenly the tunnels are a threat, not a means of escape.

What if the tunnels reach as far as Mimi's house? Could the sea rush in through a secret door while I sleep or watch cartoons on Mimi's tiny telly?

'Have you got one?' I ask, afraid to hear the answer

because if it's yes, I'll never dare to close my eyes and sleep again.

Mimi just laughs. 'Not that I know of, pet. We're a bit high above the town for tunnels.'

And for once, I'm glad to be living at the top of that steep, helter-skelter street.

Mimi checks her watch, starts packing things away in her bag. 'I might just have a few things to show you later.' She taps the side of her nose, smiles again. 'Might have a few smugglers' secrets of my own to share. Family secrets. Interested?'

I nod. 'Definitely,' I say in my Best Big Brother voice. 'Brilliant. Thank you, Mimi.'

'Now, if you want to have a quick look for fossils . . .' she says.

I glance at the sea, still sitting silver on the horizon like a sleeping sword. We don't have long; we have to leave soon for my session with Nadia. But the slipway has dried a bit while we had our sandwiches. I can risk it. I just hope Mimi can't hear my drum heart. I slide my hand along the rail as we go down, pretend to take in the view.

The sand is flat and dark and gravelly, and it doesn't try to get into my shoes like the Whitby sand. It's more like an underwater seabed than a beach and I think any minute fish will swim past my head. Green plants crawl everywhere, broken up by long thin pools stretched between seaweed-lined banks and flat stones. They're like sleeping whales or half-submerged dinosaurs. 'Watch your step on those,' Mimi says. 'They're slippery.'

Like I needed telling . . .

Mimi strides between them, over them, in her purple boots, stops and peers into a strip of seaweed-strewn water. 'Always down here, rock-pooling, when I were a lass. Caught all sorts, we did. Specially crabs and limpets.'

A tiny pink crab slides into the pool, sinks through the sand at speed, like it might recognise her.

Gone. Just like that.

A story starts writing itself in my head. Another for the book.

'See that, Jonah?' Mimi points up at the cliffs that surround the beach as far as I can see, a kind of castle wall in grey, red and green. And at the top, just above us, a tower. An actual tower, with turrets. 'That's the old watermill,' Mimi goes on. 'And it's got a story to tell too,' she says. 'Once upon a time, those smugglers used to meet there and sup their stolen whisky and make their plans. And they'd store their contraband there until the coastguard got wind of it. After that, they had several hideouts – in cellars and local fishermen's pubs. All over the place. The mill's just a hostel, these days. But if walls could talk, eh?'

I stare up at it, think of Rio and the Playmobile castle Jo bought him last Christmas. How he stared at it for hours before he put a single plastic soldier in it, because he couldn't believe it was his. Rio who would love this bay that has so many stories. Rio who wouldn't mind the sea at all, as long as it didn't steal his shoes.

I've got more important things to think about than long-dead smugglers and shore crabs. I need to work on my plan. And I need to know where Nadia is with hers – how much time I've got to change her mind. Or rescue Rio.

'Can we look for fossils another day?' I say. 'I don't want to be late for Nadia.'

CHAPTER 10

It's a new social worker at the Centre today. Not Nadia, who always smells of something that makes me sneeze, but another lady. She's the third social worker I've had. 'Nadia is away for a bit,' she says. 'She'll be back soon.' I don't ask where Nadia's gone, or why. She's probably just got tired of seeing me. But will this new social worker know about the plans for Rio?

Will she tell me?

I look at her out of the corner of my eye: side-eyed, like a fox. She has grey hair trapped down in tights plaits on the top of her head. There's a blue streak at the front, like she spilled ink there. She told me her name, but I don't remember it. I was looking at her shoes. They're red, with blue and yellow laces. Rio would love them.

I sit down in the same chair as always. The one with the squidgy orange seat that swallows you up. The one where you're supposed to talk about your feelings – and Nadia always smiles and nods and says, 'It's OK, Jonah. Just when you're ready. I'm listening.' But she's not, because even when I drag my words up from where they're hiding, she just nods and says she understands, then does what I don't want anyway.

Other times, she just nods and smiles. And that's it. Not a word except for 'well done, Jonah' and 'see you next time'.

Not-Nadia has plenty of words. Like maybe *she* doesn't like the quiet space in the room either. Her words are all round at the edges, not sort of flat and wide like people say them round here.

She's saying she knows this must feel strange, having to meet someone new. It's not. I'm used to it. People leaving. Others taking their place.

I shrug but she just carries on anyway. 'So we'll just take our time today, Jonah, get to know one another a little,' she says. 'If that's OK with you?'

My legs jiggle without my telling them to.

'You're the first Jonah I've ever met, you know,' she adds. 'Such a special name.' She stops talking and the quiet air wants to swallow me up. I try to make my legs stay still but they don't listen. I stare at the window. A few fat spatters of rain land there. Mam's face is in all of them . . .

Not-Nadia's voice makes me jump. 'Maybe you'd like to draw something today, Jonah? Or paint?' She sits down on a green plastic chair at a low table. It's meant for children, and she looks like a giant now. 'I hear you're quite an artist,' she says.

Her eyes are doing that smiling-waiting thing, so I go and sit at the opposite end of the table even though I don't want to. There's paper. A big, empty white world of it spreading in front of me. Felt tips, thin pencil crayons and fat wax crayons in glinting glass jars. Twisted tubes of paint; brushes lined up on the table, like they're waiting – expecting – something too.

Not-Nadia starts chewing her pen. She shouldn't do that. It's bad for you. She opens a drawer, takes out a small cardboard box. It rattles as she opens it. 'Have a look,' she says. 'Something here might give you an idea.'

I peer between the flaps.

There's a shell.

It's all I see.

The outside is rough and spiky. I can already hear the sea inside it, smell the salt air caught there. I shake my head.

Not-Nadia takes out some bright beads, a bent silver coin, a small bear, a tiny blue shoe, a large marble – swirls of yellow and gold inside it. A curled skeleton leaf, a magnifying glass with a scratched silver handle, and the shell.

I know why *they're* there: the shell and the marble. She wants me to talk about Whitby. About Mam. About Rio – losing them both.

I *can't* ask my question. The answer might swallow me like the sea.

I need to get out of here, work on my own plans for Rio.

Not-Nadia turns the shell upside down on the table, peers at it, like she's surprised to find it there. I want to push it out of sight, but I steel myself, pick it up, turn it around and stare into the shiny pink inner coil. It's like a tunnel. Or a throat. Like the shell's not an abandoned home, but a living thing, mouth gaping. I smell its sea-breath, hold my own. I hope Not-Nadia can't tell.

She writes something on her paper pad. Her writing is scratchy and loud. She smiles again, opens the box of felt tips slowly, as if there's treasure inside; moves them towards me. My legs keep on jiggling. My hands don't want to move. I bite my lip. Taste salt. Think of the shell again. The Whitby sea. Mam. Rio.

I try to find Jonah the Brave. He's not here.

The white paper on the table stares back at me, and my arms gets heavier and heavier. I've got to draw *something*, just so I can go. Then Not-Nadia can stare at my picture and search for clues – try to see what has spilled out on to the paper from inside me so she can agree about Rio being better off without me forever, just like Mam obviously is. I look at the red felt tip. I think of scribbling my red angry self all over the white paper, covering every inch of it; scribbling over the edges, over the table, over the stupid beige walls.

Or I could find the black one, draw the big, empty, falling space in the middle of me. The space where I'm supposed to be Rio's big brother.

I don't know the colour for scared.

Not-Nadia gets up and stands over by the window. I know why she's doing that, but it won't help. She won't find any Bad-Luck Jonah in anything I draw; nothing to help her sit in another meeting and nod her head and decide things about my life. The real Jonah's hidden away, trapped down tight like Not-Nadia's inky plaits. Disappeared. Like Mam.

Not-Nadia starts chasing the raindrops down the glass with her finger, like I do when I'm bored. I can tell by the squeak. I pretend to make more room, push the shell behind the box so I can't see it any more. I scan the line of pencil crayons. Black's not there anyway. It never is. And the red needs sharpening.

Come on, Jonah. Just draw something. Anything. Then you can leave.

I think of the fox. Her red-flag coat. I squeeze my eyes shut and I see hers again, fixed on mine for a long moment: star-bright, yellow swirled with gold. A jolt of electricity runs through me. That fox, she *means* something. But what?

My hand itches to draw her. I run it across the white paper world in front of me.

But no. I'm keeping the fox for myself. For me, and for Rio.

A pigeon lands on the window ledge, its grey-blue colours blurring against the wet glass as if it's slowly dissolving, melting away like coloured ice.

I tip the pencil crayons on to the table and search for its disappearing colours.

Part of me disappears into the drawing, like always, and that's good because it smooths out the edges of the cut-glass sadness in my stomach – just a bit – and stops the hands on the clock creeping slow, slow, slow. When I'm done, I sit back, fold my arms and the pigeon's black bead eye stares up from the page from inside a muddle of colours.

'W*onderful*, Jonah. Thank you,' Not-Nadia says. I wait for her to put it in the file that has my name on the front and is all about me even though I've never seen it, and no one's asked me if anything inside it is true. My bottom hovers above the tiny chair, my eyes are on the door.

But she sits down next to me again. I stay hovering, ready to run like a smuggler in the bay if she starts talking about stories hidden in the picture, trying to steal my secrets.

But she's asking me if I'd like to give the picture to Rio. Telling me we're going to see him – today – in a bit. That Mimi rang, and something about it being time, and I can't listen properly past the fizz in the middle of me, and the stories *I'm* seeing behind her words.

Rio missing me too much, and social workers changing their minds. Me going home – to Jo's – with Rio. Rio in Mimi's blue bubble car, coming to live with me in her wonky house. Mam, here to take us both back where we belong.

I nod so hard my head nearly falls off and I'm up from the chair and by the door and Not-Nadia is saying, 'Whoa, slow down, Jonah. We've a bit of time yet.'

She gets me a glass of squash and it stings my tongue, but I drink it all because nothing matters except seeing Rio. I grab the box of felt tips, curl my arm around a new sheet of paper, like Rio always does, and this time I draw our fox.

CHAPTER 11

Rio's walking towards me across the park and my heart is too big for my chest. Someone's cut his hair all wrong. He's holding Nadia's hand, because she's not sick, or tired, she's just his social worker now and not mine because 'it's best we have one each now, just for us'. That pours water on my firework fizz, and I can't listen to Not-Nadia's explanation in the car because I'm gripping tight hold of my new stories. Splitting social workers doesn't fit.

Rio's feet are trailing, scuffing like when he's tired or when Mam got him second-hand wellies three sizes too big for him.

I run up to him. 'Hi, Big Man,' I say.

He sinks down inside his jacket collar and sways from side to side and *he won't look at me.*

Mimi's hand is on my shoulder. She stoops down in front of Rio. 'Lovely swings over there, Rio. Want a push?'

He lifts his chin. His eyes dart sideways. Rio, he loves swings. 'Red one,' he mumbles, sliding his chin back inside his coat. He looks up at Nadia, like she's in charge of him now, doesn't rush off across the park like *my* Rio would do.

Nadia sits down on a bench; nods, smiles. 'It's OK, Rio,' she whispers, even though nothing feels OK at all, and I want to scream at her because that's another lie, and she's stolen Rio's colours and made him afraid of me.

I feel like I'm shrinking too, inside myself, because my happy stories are floating away like pages snatched by the wind. But Rio's only four. I have to be Jonah the Best Big Brother who makes things right. So I grin and say, 'Race you for the red one, Rio,' because he hates losing and red is his favourite. I pretend to trip, let him win.

He wriggles backwards on to the swing. I push and push and push until my arms ache. 'High as the sky, Jonah,' he shouts. 'Up to the moon.'

His bubble-laugh comes, floats down to the ground, lifts back in the air as he swings. His Rio colours are back. I want to keep him flying forever, so they never leave. But after a few minutes, Jo says it's time for ice cream – something else Rio loves – and he's too little to know that means she's getting ready to take him away from me again. He chooses a rainbow rocket lolly from the van. I have the same even though I'd prefer a cornet with a flake on top.

The ice-cream man has snow-white hair under his cap and curly white eyebrows, and as I unwrap his lolly, Rio asks if that's because he eats ice cream every day.

We sit on the grass and Rio stares at his lolly like it's the most beautiful thing he's ever seen. He sails it in the air, makes it fly to the moon, 'like Rio on the swing'.

The sun comes out, like it's just for him, and red and pink and green ice runs down his arm, drips from his fingers. He laughs again and his rocket slides from the stick and crashes on the ground in a rainbow puddle.

'Gone,' he says. His eyes are sudden puddles too. His bottom lip wobbles and wobbles, so I give him the rest of my lolly.

'Eat it quickly, this time,' I say, 'or the sun might steal that one too.'

He pushes it in his mouth and his eyes get rounder and rounder because it's cold, cold, cold.

'I made you a whole book,' I say. 'With stories *and* pictures. Did you get it yet?'

His nods, smiles around his lolly, letting more melting ice escape. 'The Octopus is best,' says. 'It's naughty.'

He wipes his sleeve across his mouth, stares at the remains of his rocket. 'Want you to read it to me,' he mutters. 'Not Jo.'

'I know, Big Man,' I say, past the roadblock in my throat. 'I will. Soon.'

He hands the empty lolly stick to me without looking up. I slide it into my pocket. Out of the corner of my eye, I notice Jo and Mimi, watching us. Nadia is on her feet now.

I want to stretch our time together and make him smile again, so I tell him about the fox with her red-flag coat and marble eyes and how she's come to tell us something. I take the picture from my pocket and hold it out to him. It's all creased, and I see that I've given her one ear bigger than the other. I wish I'd drawn it better. Rio strokes the paper fox with his fingers like its real. 'Rio's fox too,' he says. He folds it carefully, the tip of his tongue poking out as he presses along each fold with a sticky thumb.

Mimi comes and sits beside me. 'Time to say goodbye for now, Jonah,' she says, and brushes hair from my eyes.

My story pages tumble to the ground like dead birds and it feels like my heart falls with them. No one's changed their minds about anything.

Rio tugs on Mimi's sleeve and she stoops, puts her face closer to his. His words spill out like pencils tipped from a packet, clattering into the held-breath quiet air. 'Can I come and live at your house too? I only small and Jonah likes me sleeping in his bed and I won't keep dropping ice cream or screaming and I don't eat lots of food.'

Nadia steps in. 'We talked about that, didn't we, Rio?'

Rio shakes his head. 'Didn't,' he says.

And I know he's right because it's always other people that talk about things, and me and Rio don't get to say anything about what we want.

On the way back across the park, Rio's hand snakes inside mine. 'The sea stole my yellow sandal, didn't it, Jonah?' he says in a too-loud whisper.

I nod, hold my breath.

'Want it back now,' he whispers. 'Please, Jonah.'

My throat squeezes so tight no words can get out. My feet are heavy, heavy, slow just like Rio's all the way back to Nadia's car. Because Rio doesn't care about his sandal. He wants Mam and he wants his big brother and I HAVE to make that happen. Fast.

'Don't worry, Big Man,' I tell him. 'Everything will be OK. I'm working on it. And you know what, maybe our fox will help us. You just look after her picture for me, all right, until you come and meet her for yourself.'

He nods but he's already faded, begun to disappear like the pigeon behind the rainy windowpane.

He kicks and shouts when Nadia lifts him into the car. His hands press against the window, two trapped butterflies on the glass, and my promises to him dissolve into a puddle, splatted and useless like his first-ever rainbow-ice rocket.

There's less time than I thought. Rio's already unravelling without me.

I need a better rescue plan.

And for some reason, I can't shake the feeling that the fox knows something that can help me.

CHAPTER 12

I watch for her wherever we go.

It's another week before I see her. And this time, she's following someone.

I'm standing by the car, waiting for Mimi, who 'popped to the postbox', and is now talking to a girl in a green jacket by the entrance to the car park. Mimi. She knows *everyone*.

They're down on the sand: the fox and – a smallish person in a cap. The slipway is dry today, so I move a bit closer, grip the railings and peer over. 'No further without me, mind, Jonah,' Mimi calls. Which is good, because it means I've hidden my fear of the sea from her, like I wanted. But bad, because she's keeping her eye on me like I'm four, doesn't let me out of her sight.

The sun is low, just sitting above the line of the sea and making silver splinters on the surface. I squint and shield my eyes with one hand to see better.

The small person is a boy – I think. It's hard to be sure. Whoever it is has quite long hair, lifting from underneath the cap, in the breeze from the sea. He – and the fox – are right down on the shoreline. Where the waves are lapping. I feel them: cold and creeping back and forth, back and forth, over their feet. A fraction further each time. A little bit higher. I shiver, take a step backwards.

The boy and the fox are a few metres apart and both seem to be searching for something. She keeps her nose to the sand, lifts a foot every now and then, pauses with it in mid-air, like a dancer. He walks slowly, bending like one of those skinny-legged, long-beaked beach birds. Every now and again, he pokes at the sand. The two of them take no notice of one another. Might not even know the other is there. But it's like they're fastened together by an invisible rope, moving in time with one another, still at the same moments.

My stomach twists. The fox is mine. Mine and Rio's.

It should be me. A new Jonah: Jonah the Brave – dancing with a wild fox – skirting the tide, staring in the face of the sea. Writing new stories in the sand. With Rio.

The fox freezes, tail stretched out behind her like an arrow. The boy looks up – no: *stares* upwards at the sky, stuffs something in a bag at his belt, turns towards the slipway. Is he leaving?

I check over my shoulder. Mimi's fishing in her bag for

something. 'Just coming,' she calls. Like she can see me even when she's looking somewhere else. Not like Mam, who hardly seemed to see me when I was right in front of her. I turn back towards the beach.

The sea is closer still. Already. Like it pushes forward every time I turn my back. Like in the game that makes Rio scream-laugh, where I have to be Mr Wolf again, again, again and try to 'eat him all up'. I hear his giggle and my eyes get wet. I squeeze them tight shut. When I open them, the fox and the boy are nowhere to be seen.

Are they *both* hiding out in the caves?

On the drive home, I spot the Whitby bus again. That might be part of a Plan C (desperate measures) if I need one.

It's parked outside a pub called the Smugglers' Arms. I ask Mimi if the bus goes all the way to Jo's house – 'For when I'm allowed visit Rio by myself,' I say.

She looks at me narrow-eyed like her cat does, only kinder, and I need to be more careful because maybe she can hear things I'm not saying. Her fingers get tighter on the steering wheel, and she suggests we 'have another chat about Rio when we're home, Jonah, love.' The words she's *not* saying make the air in the car thick and heavy even though I don't know what they are.

When she does say them, it's worse than I thought. I don't care about the stupid fox or the stupid boy or Mimi's stupid family secrets any more. It's too late for any of them.

Nadia has new parents for Rio. Already. Or she thinks she does. They've chosen him in that stupid online magazine, and if another meeting – an Adoption Panel – says it's a good idea, they'll be able to meet him soon and then there'll be a few more weeks of getting to know one another . . . So I've got to wait another month to see him again, so I don't 'unsettle him' before they do. Before he meets STRANGERS. And I'M HIS BROTHER!

I can't find Jonah the Brave. Or Jonah the Best Big Brother.

I'M THUNDER AND LIGHTNING. I'M THE HISSING, SPITTING SEA.

I thunder up the stairs and thunder back down again and I'm out of the front door and I'm running, running, running. I go up, up, up, not down, down towards the sea, and my breathing tears my chest. Makes. Sword-stabs. In. My. Side. Walls and windows and waving trees whisk by like a speeded-up film until I've no idea where I am and I don't care, I don't care, I don't care . . .

I might be sick.

I stop. Bend double on the pavement. A door creaks open. Shoes. No, slippers. Large red ones. I look up, gulping for air, and Slipper-Man says, 'You OK, son?' And I wipe my nose on my sleeve and run, run, run again until there's no air left to breathe and I have to stop.

There's an alleyway between two of the houses. Narrow and cobbled, like always round here. Trees peep over the wall. Something with pointy leaves and curly stems pokes through cracks wherever it can. Escaping. Like me.

I don't want any more slipper-people with their questions, so I run halfway down the alley, slide down against the wall. The running has made my tears loose and they start escaping too, dripping off the end of my nose. A jagged noise comes up through my throat and this time I know I'm breaking apart inside and the only thing worse is that Rio might be too. When these new parents meet him, they'll want him. Anyone would. Will Not-Nadia or Mimi even *tell* me when they're taking him? Or where? The new mam and dad will probably break promises too, and we'll never, ever see one another again.

My head is stone-heavy in my hands. I'm cold. Turning solid like the fossils in the bay. I might as well have written my own promise to Rio in the sand, with a stick.

My heart is a drum again. I've just made things ten times worse. Running off – smashing things – that's the red-scribble Jonah. The Jonah who can't be a big brother any more and won't even be allowed 'visits' with Rio when he's been stolen by these 'new parents'.

Mimi will have called Not-Nadia, reported me 'absent without leave'. Like the soldiers we learned about in school, who got so scared and tired of guns and bombs and losing their 'brothers' that their legs made them run away too, even though they were much, much braver than me.

Maybe, if I *was* brave, I'd leave Rio alone. Let him have his new family that might have a mam and a dad that don't disappear. Maybe a new big brother too. One that's not afraid of anything. One that's not bad luck and doesn't keep letting him down. My insides twist and twist like the seaweed on the beach and they hurt, hurt, hurt . . .

I shouldn't have run away.

Dark spots on the ground. Cold spatters in my hair. Like the sky is crying too.

I have to get back. Say sorry.

I stand up. Which way?

I creep along the alley, arms clutching my stomach. I slide my shoes slipper-soft in case anyone is there. I keep close to the wall, peer round as it bends to the left and then there's a tiny street full of tiny houses with miniscule front gardens. They're still climbing up, up, not sliding towards the sea. There's another alleyway, this one surrounded by thick green hedges on both sides. I creep alongside it. Halfway down, someone – or something – has pushed through, leaving a jagged gap in the branches.

Sudden footsteps close by, clatter-clattering to get out of the rain, and what will the owner say about a boy with no coat lurking in an alley in the rain? I'm not waiting to find out. I squeeze though the gap, eyes tight shut because there might be someone on the other side as well and I don't want to know. Scratchy twig fingers catch at my sleeve and my cheeks, tug on the leg of my jeans to stop me. But I'm through.

I crouch under a bush, and it drip-drips water down my neck. There's a hole in my sweatshirt sleeve and Mimi will probably be mad about that too, like Mam. Because 'money don't grow on trees, Jonah' and 'why can't you be more careful?' I roll up my sleeve in case I forget to do it later.

I'm in a garden – or rather lots of gardens all together with no fences in between. There are long strips of soil and tiny plants lined up like they're on parade. There are sticks, with little flag-labels drooping in the wet air, glass boxes with misty sides so I can't see what's inside. And – one, two, three, four, five sheds with pointed roofs and coloured doors. One of them is leaning like it might be about to give up, and they all look old and faded – except for one with a bright blue door.

The rain is rattling like bullets through the leaves now. I'm getting cold, cold, cold. And I still don't know where I am or how to get home. The sky pushes grey clouds around, rolls them over the last of the daylight. I think it hates me just like the Whitby sea and I should shelter somewhere better, in case it gets even angrier. But I've got no chance of getting home once it gets dark, so I don't know what to do. It's all a muddle in my head. I curl up in a ball under the useless bush umbrella. And all I can think of is Rio, who gets scared in case lightning comes when it rains and doesn't have me to tell him it's just the sky getting ready to make a rainbow. Rio who makes me brave, even though I'm scared too. I curl around my stomach, which is hurting even more than my heart.

Come on, Jonah.

I wipe my sleeve across my eyes; uncurl.

Golden eyes through the stripes of rain.

Flame-red face, pointed ears, white chin; peering out from the side of the blue-door shed.

The fox. *Our* fox. Mine and Rio's.

She's back.

She lifts her head, sniffs the air. She can smell me.

She shakes rain from her whiskers.

She sees me.

Her shoulders drop a little and she freezes and it's just like my dream with window-eyes burning into mine. We're both statue-still. She lifts one ballerina front foot, then the other. Her legs are black almost to the knees, like she's wearing boots. She eases forward, stretches out her neck, nose twitching. I hold my breath and freeze my body still. I'm an explorer staring through jungle vines, face to face with a tiger, and I really am Jonah the Brave.

Closer, closer, she creeps, like it's a film and someone slowed it down. I can see diamond-drops on her whiskers. I'm her prey and she's stalking me, capturing me with her eyes . . .

She just stares and stares and tilts her head. She doesn't blink. I try to do the same in case the drop-flick of my eyelids breaks the spell; shatters the moment like glass; spills me back out of her wild-fox world into the one where I'm alone and scared and no one seems to see me at all.

The creak-slam of a door.

The fox is gone. Torn away in a tail-flick fluster of red,

black and white even before I see that someone else is there, standing in the doorway of the blue shed.

Before she's had the chance to tell me why she's here.

CHAPTER 13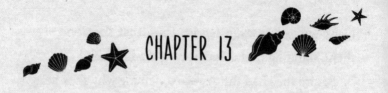

It's a boy, dressed in a yellow plastic coat that's so big I can just see the toes of his green wellies. But even with his hair plastered down by the rain, and no cap, I know it's him.

Beach-Bird-Boy. The one that danced with my fox. He's stolen her away again.

'Blimey,' he says. He opens the door again, tilts his head towards it. I shake my head, sending raindrops flying from my hair, because he's stolen Jonah the Brave too: I don't know him, not really, and you don't go into sheds with strangers, even boy-sized ones.

'Fine,' he says. 'If you don't mind getting struck by lightning as well as half drowned.'

He ducks back inside the shed and the sky cracks and flashes like he made it happen, so I scuttle after him and slam the door shut. I keep hold of the handle, just in case, because why has he invited me in when he doesn't know me, and I have basically broken into his garden? He takes a pair of glasses from his pocket, wipes them on a rag and puts them on.

'You're Jonah,' he says, and my heart does a frog leap because I must already be on the TV news, in a police announcement, and everyone is searching for me and that's how Beach-Bird-Boy knows. Which means I'm IN EVEN BIGGER TROUBLE than I thought, for wasting people's time.

My mouth does a fish impression, but no words come out. Beach-Bird-Boy just clears some plant pots from a battered old chair, pats his chest and says, 'Freddie. Remember? Sit down if you want to.'

So I do, because my legs are thinking of folding up anyway. Freddie-Who-Thinks-He-Knows-Me takes off his giant raincoat and leans back against a wooden bench, rests his elbows careful-slow between plastic trays full of tar-black soil. I must be still doing my goldfish gawp because he smiles, goes on.

'Saw you that day in school – in the dinner hall. With Ms Mukherjee . . .?'

I nod, and close my mouth, like I do remember. But I'm just seeing eyes everywhere, hands covering whispers, hearing clattering feet and clattering chairs. Remembering the way my mouth didn't work that day, how everyone prob'ly thought I was weird, or stuck-up, or stupid. How they must've guessed Mimi wasn't my mam.

Good job I'm not going back there.

Another crack of thunder. The wind howls around the shed like its arguing with it, forces its way under the door and presses my soaked sweatshirt against my skin. My teeth chatter so Freddie will think I'm scared. But Rio is in my head, hands over his ears, asking if our house is made of bricks, so a wolf wouldn't be able to blow it down. That day, being Jonah the Brave was easy.

My voice rushes back up my throat from wherever it's been hiding. 'I wasn't doing anything. I mean, I didn't know I was in your garden. I just, I just . . . I got lost and it was raining, and . . . Sorry, I've got to go now.'

Freddie does his head-on-one-side-like-a-bird thing again. 'I'd wait a bit if I was you,' he says. 'Storm's still right overhead.' He shakes soil from a checked blanket and hands it to me. 'And it's an allotment,' he says. 'Not a garden. My dad's allotment. Well, this bit around our shed is his anyway.' He reaches for one of the plastic trays, tilts it to show me tiny green shoots peeping out of the soil. He lifts a miniscule leaf with one finger. 'I was going to plant these out for him, but the rain's too heavy, so . . .'

I stare at the spindly stems, wonder what they are and why Freddie's so bothered about them. Why he's being nice. Why his dad's making him work in this garden and whether he's going to appear any minute to collect Freddie and go ballistic about having a runaway in his shed.

'He can't,' Freddie says, when I ask if he's coming. 'He's working late.' And it's like the weather changes suddenly in his face too, so I don't ask my other questions. Pebbles of rain bounce off the windows, rattle on the tin roof. I picture the shed floating on the sea like a tiny ark and I'm glad we're high up, well away from the bay, even if I still have no idea how to get home. I wish Freddie hadn't sent the fox away because maybe she has a hideout somewhere warm and dry and she'd lead me there, let me curl up next to her. Then I'd become wild and brave and clever like she is.

His eyes are on me again. He definitely reads thoughts.

'Storm will ease up soon,' he says. 'Want me to walk you into town? I'm going to the Spar on my way home. I could walk you that far. If you know the way to your house from there?' He shrugs. 'If you want . . .?'

I say, 'Yes, please,' because wild foxes don't really make friends with people, even small ones and I need to 'stop making up stupid stories and get real', like mam says. And because, to be fair, Freddie-Fox-Thief hasn't once asked me why I'm out like this, with no coat, a snotty nose and puffy, crybaby eyes.

'It's not my house,' I hear myself say. 'I'm just staying there for a bit. Till my mam's better.'

Freddie just nods and says, 'Everyone knows Mimi. She's all right.' And if his bird-eyes can spot half-truths as well, he doesn't let on.

CHAPTER 14

The storm blows out as quickly as it blew in, like Freddie said it would. It's getting dark now, and round every corner I wait for the sweep of torches, searching lines of police, social workers and shopkeepers. Maybe even dogs with sniffing noses and drooling jaws. My jeans drag heavy with water, stick to my cold legs, so the hilly streets seem steeper than ever. It's like we're climbing into the sky and it's pressing down on us, pushing us back where we've come from. I can't get enough air in my lungs to breathe and talk at the same time. I keep stopping and bending over because the knife is back between my ribs, so Freddie has to stop too, and he could be at the shop by now. He doesn't seem to mind, just waits, takes out his phone, making a tiny blue star in the nearly-darkness.

I know when we're getting close to the town because the hiss of the sea threads inside the wind and the swish-splatter of rain. Freddie tells me the weather's settling. Either there's something wrong with his hearing, or he's just trying to cheer me up because he knows there'll be another kind of storm when I get to Mimi's.

Thinking about that puts spikes in my stomach again. But there are questions pressing there too, and if I don't ask them now, I probably won't get another chance. They burst out with my puffing breath just as we pass the museum with its dark windows. 'Did you see the fox in your garden – allotment? What were you doing together down on the beach, and is it your pet and isn't that against the law, and what happens if Pest Control sees it, and shouldn't you let it go back to its wild home? To its family . . .'

A car struggles past on the slippery steep street. It's not Mimi's blue bubble car, or a striped police vehicle with its siren off, pretending. Freddie waits for the huff of its engine and splashing of its tyres to stop. 'Oh no,' he says. 'Fox back again, was she?' He sighs, shoves his hands deep into his plastic pockets, and he tells me his own fox story as we walk on . . .

He found her under his shed, just a small cub, winter-thin and terrified by the snap-bang-boom of November fireworks. He wanted to tuck her up in the warmth of his shed, muffle the sounds with blankets, but her sharp teeth said NO and so did his dad. 'Because she's wild, Freddie, and the wild has its own ways and locking her in a wooden box would terrify her more, make her wither away. Just leave her be,' he'd said. 'And besides, foxes are vermin to some people, and you can't encourage them. If the allotment folk get wind of us keeping a fox in that shed, they'll call in Pest Control, for sure, and we'll lose the allotment. And the fox would end up – well, the fox would END. Right there.'

Freddie brings out his blue-star phone again, checks the screen. The tap-tap of his fingers is LOUD and I realise that the weather has quieted, just like he said it would. Like it's been listening to his fox story too.

He drops the phone back into his pocket, snuffs out the star. He tells me how *he* didn't listen – to his dad – because the fox's eyes were begging, and she was small and scared; how he saved part of his school sandwiches each day, sneaked scraps of meat and fish from his weekend dinner plates, poked them under the shed. How she never came near, not even for the food, until he was gone. How he would drop in on her on his way to school some mornings, watch her scamper back under the shed, belly rounder now, coat reddening in the early sun.

How one morning, a pest controller came too, with his net and stick, his sharp warnings when he couldn't catch her; the sharp words from Freddie's dad and the twist in Freddie's stomach because he'd lied and let him down.

'The fox, she kept away for a few weeks,' Freddie said, 'and I thought maybe she'd moved on somewhere safer. But she turned up again with the Christmas snows, thinner than ever, just as people were digging up their carrots and sprouts, clearing drifts from their patches.'

We're by the bakery now, where I first saw the fox, hungry still. I picture her back then on Freddie's allotment: a Christmas red alert in that frozen white-out, hunger biting at her, forcing her back into the danger zone. And I'm back in my old life too, with the bitter nip of snow-cold toes in broken trainers, me and Rio huddled under our night-time blanket, smoke-breath in the bedroom and no coins for the meter. No mam.

Poor fox.

Freddie hasn't finished his story. I can't see his face properly, but his voice sounds like worry, worry, worry now. I listen above the sea-wind whine, and it makes me forget the waiting Mimi storm. My brain whirs because maybe I need a fox-escape plan now too . . . but then who's rescuing who?

Freddie started seeing her on the beach, so thought if he fed her down there, in one of the caves – made a kind

96

of den for her – she'd keep away from the shed, from the allotments. Just until the spring weather when she was old enough to fend for herself – find easy food.

I nod, and droplets of rain run from my hair and down my nose. 'Good idea,' I say. And I like this Beach-Bird-Boy Freddie a bit more, even though he might have stolen my fox.

Freddie shrugs. 'Not sure now,' he says. 'If she was back by the shed today. People are saying she's hanging round town too. And if she's still doing that and wandering along the beach at Easter, when the tourists come . . .' He sighs. 'Maybe I've just made things worse.'

He hasn't, though, because a warm cave and food every day is better than cold and wet and an empty stomach. Better than no one even noticing. *That's* worse.

I can't tell him that. But I wish I could.

'I never spoke to her, though,' he says. 'Never encouraged her close. So she'd stay wild and remember humans aren't safe. She keeps well back from me. So that's something.'

'Oh,' I say. 'Right.' And I don't tell him about earlier, either. About the black quivering nose and rain-crystal whiskers. The hot fox breath on my face, the golden eyes staring into mine as I crawled from the hedge. *My fox,* after all, perhaps . . .

The Spar windows are dark, covered by steel blinds. A note fights with the wind like a battered bird, flutters by a last corner of sticky tape on the door:

CLOSED EARLY DUE TO STORM.
OPENS 7.30 A.M.

Freddie needed to buy stuff and now he can't and that's my fault for walking too slowly. He stares at the door as if it might change its mind, swing open and let him in. 'Oh,' is all he says, but his face is hiding more words, and maybe his stomach will be snake-bite empty tonight, because my bad luck has spilled on to him.

I think of Mimi's kitchen cupboards, full to bursting like a small shop of her own. The basket on the table crammed with bright green apples, purple grapes and huge banana claws. 'Mimi could give you something for tea,' I tell Freddie. 'She won't mind,' I add, even though she's probably going to mind everything after what I've done, and there might be police officers on the doorstep and Freddie will know I'm trouble.

But Freddie just shakes his head, says, 'It's OK,' and, 'I'll sort something for tea, and I'd best get going 'cos

Dad will be home soon. If you're sure you're all right from here, Jonah?'

I nod, even though that's true and not true, and I wish 'thank you' sounded bigger.

'See you, Jonah,' he says, and the dim side alley snatches him away.

I climb back up through the wonky streets towards the sky and Mimi, wondering what it's like to have a dad, where Freddie's mam is, and why Freddie has to do the shopping and make the tea and look after his dad's allotment as well.

Whether *he* has a little brother to look out for too.

CHAPTER 15

Mimi's street is velvet-black except for bright jewel windows where people have forgotten to close their curtains. A brown dog barks through the glass because I am a stranger walking past his house, and I'd 'better not come any nearer'. A family are sitting round a table: a girl in a highchair, a boy about the same age as me. A man: a dad. Another dad sits down next to the girl, and I wonder how come some children get two dads and me and Rio don't even get one. My insides feel colder than ever and I think maybe it's always winter in Robin Hood's Bay.

Mimi's windows are dark. My heartbeats panic because she's out with the police like I thought. I don't have a key. And I can't tell her I'm back and I'm sorry . . .

Footstep-scuffles on the pavement. Two figures hurrying round the corner towards me, torches making moon sweeps on the fences, on the pavement. On purple boots.

It's Mimi, bag swinging from her arm like always. With someone she knows. Like always. Whoever it is will see the Mimi-storm, tell everyone she doesn't know how Mimi puts up with a red-scribble boy like me . . .

I hold my breath, brace myself for loud words that jump and sting and hurt my ears. But Mimi swooshes towards me in a gush of wet wool and words as soft as sighs. Her arms are wide wings like she wants to hug me, so my bones go stiff because no one hugs me except Rio. I step back.

Mimi says, 'Sorry, sorry, Jonah. Here you are, back then! Thank the Lord for that. Let's get you inside.'

Her key flashes silver in the torchlight, trembles a bit. The doorway paints a yellow hole in the dark and we step inside it. Three of us, squashed together in Mimi's narrow hall, all elbows and water droplets, struggling out of our wet coats and boots.

A woman: small, like Mimi, hangs a rain-spattered grey coat next to Mimi's, like she lives here too. The stranger. What's she doing coming in?

She might feel me glaring at her because she smiles, and it's Mimi's face: except her cheeks are rounder and her skin is darker – a bit like mine. Unless it's just the light in the hallway.

101

'This is my sister Lois,' Mimi tells me. 'She'll be dying for a cuppa...'

Lois smiles. Her smile is nearly Mimi's smile. 'You bet,' she says. 'Get that kettle on, sis.' She unwinds a long scarf from her head, and it twists around her shoulders in a bright puddle.

I follow her and Mimi through to the warm kitchen, with the knives back in my stomach because Mimi must keep her storms for indoors. My ears stretch for the sharp knock of police knuckles on the front door, the rumble and door-slam of Not-Nadia's car, come to take me goodness knows where.

Lois plonks herself down in Mimi's chair, drapes the scarf over the wooden arms and it hangs like striped snakeskin. Its colours sing like Rio's name. I can't take my eyes off her because her hair isn't Mimi's hair, with its straight spikes and silver streaks. It's tight to her head in black wiry curls. It's like mine.

Mimi takes a towel from the Aga, drapes it around my shoulders. 'Let's get a warm drink down you, lad, then it's a nice hot bath for you before anything else,' she says.

I rub the towel over my hair, wrap my hands around the warm mug she hands me, try not to think about the 'anything else' that's coming after my bath. Chocolate steam mists my face. I try not to notice the secret look Mimi gives Lois so that she gets up as soon as she's drained her own mug. This is it, then . . .

'Best be off. Nice to meet you, Jonah,' Lois says. She winds the rainbow snake back around her head like a kind of turban. Mimi walks her to the front door and I catch their broken whispers, try to piece together what they're saying.

Then Mimi's quick steps are on the stairs and water thunders in the pipes. 'Bath's nearly ready, pet,' Mimi says as she comes back into the kitchen. 'Then we'll have a chat.'

But waiting is just stretching the worry like tight string around my chest, and it SNAPS right then. My sorrys spill out in a rush like when Rio threw up tuna pasta all over his yellow flip-flops and I'm sobbing and my nose and eyes are spilling out too.

Mimi sits down next to me with a box of tissues, and she does the waiting instead of me. After a bit, she says, 'That's it. Let it all out, Jonah. Better out than in.' She puts her hand on my arm and I let her because I feel as if I'm breaking into pieces and her arm is solid; might stop me floating away like torn paper.

'I understand, you know, lad,' Mimi says. 'And if you think your social worker's about to turn up and whisk you away, stop you ever seeing your brother again, you're wrong. I did let her know you'd run off – I had to. There are rules for foster carers too. To help keep children safe. But I said, "Give it an hour or two because Jonah's a sensible lad, and he'll be back." Which you were. *Are*.' She smiles the smile she shares with her sister. 'Then Lois and I did a little recce of our own. Just to be on the safe side . . . and you turned up just in the nick of time. Two hours exactly, you were gone!' She squeezes my arm. 'I do need to know where you were. What you did, please. When you're ready, Jonah.'

The she leaps up like someone stuck a pin in her, because, 'Oh no! The bath's running! What am I like?' She clatters up and down the stairs to 'save the ceiling from falling in'. She makes more hot chocolate to have in the bath, with a fat toasted teacake to go with it, 'because there aren't any rules about that whatever anyone says'. She tells me that Not-Nadia will come by tomorrow for a chat, but not for a telling-off and not to take me away, because she'd have to get past *her* first. My mouth twitches with a smile because Mimi is nearly small enough to step over, but then I think maybe she's tougher than she looks. And that today she was on my side.

That makes me feel a tiny bit braver.

CHAPTER 16

The bath is deep and warm and like sinking into a different world that's safer and a bit like one of Rio's hugs. I stay in it until there are little bumps on my arms and knees, and Mimi is knocking on the door saying, 'Supper's on the table,' so I can't put off 'the chat' any longer.

Mimi's made hot salty chips, and eggs like golden eyes that remind me of the fox. I eat so quickly my tongue stings, even though I thought my stomach was too full of worry.

When I'm done, she slides some of her own chips on to my plate – the best, crispiest ones. I think my cheeks go pink because it's usually me leaving my best bits for Rio. No one does that for me. Mimi just smiles her smile, says, 'You're welcome, Jonah.'

Being full of chips makes my words slide up and out. And telling her about earlier is easier than I thought because Mimi knows Freddie.

She beams, nods her head. 'Smashing lad, Frederic.

Happy to help anybody. His dad was always like that too.'

I store up the 'was' in my head because it feels heavy with something sad. Or important. But I do ask about his mam.

'Went back home – overseas. America, I think,' Mimi says. 'A long time ago now . . .' But this time her lips close together in a full stop, so I store that for later too, with a big 'IMPORTANT' label in my head because the sea has stolen Freddie's mam too, and maybe he was searching for clues that day I saw him in the bay . . .

'Lovely little family, Tomas and Freddie Nowak. How lucky you stumbled into that allotment. We'll have to invite Freddie for his tea or something. Say a proper thank you.'

My insides nip because if Freddie comes round for tea, he'll find out things and won't want to be friends with me any more. But I like Mimi a little bit right then because she knows that two people make a family and you don't need more, so I smile.

She shifts in her seat. Her eyes are holding mine now, soft and still like the fox's eyes earlier. 'Thanks to Freddie, you're home safe this time, Jonah. And none the worse for disappearing off like that. But promise me, now, no more running away. You can be angry here in this house with me. You can shout and scream and cry and tell it like it is right here. These old walls can take it.' She smiles but her eyes stay serious. 'And so can I.'

I nod. 'Sorry,' I say, and I want to tell her how my red-scribble feelings push my arms and legs around before I can stop them, but my words are stuck again, swallowed down with the chips and egg.

Mimi pats my hand. 'I've got something that might help when you feel angry or upset, Jonah. Out back,' she says. 'But it'll have to be for tomorrow.' She gets up and slides the plates into the tiny dishwasher. It clunks and swooshes like an old steam engine. 'Now,' she says, 'how about we take a peek at those family secrets before bed? And for that, we need my grandad's box . . .'

'Grandad's box' lives in an old desk with legs that twist like the candy canes on Scarborough Pier. I hadn't noticed the desk before, tucked away under the stairs, and I didn't like looking at it now, because it was covered in frames with pictures of Mimi's family; so many they were nearly falling off the ends. I thought of my Life Story book and the torn-bird photos of Mam, wished my red-scribble fingers had left them be, so that I could put them in frames too. Maybe.

Mimi pressed something on the left-hand side of the

desk. A small drawer slid open. A secret compartment. She fished inside, brought out a tiny black key. 'Hold this a minute, Jonah,' she says and drops it into my hand. It's light as air but I feel the press of years of secrets and stories in my palm.

Mimi opens a deeper drawer, lifts out a black metal box. One of its corners is bashed in and there are scratches on the lid. 'Go on, then. Open it up,' Mimi says. 'Grandad wouldn't mind . . .'

The key turns first time with a click that jumps up into my fingers. The lid is stiff, and Mimi puts the box on my lap so I can prise it open with both hands. I peer inside.

Maybe I was expecting gold coins or smugglers' knives or something, but there are just crumpled papers with curly writing, two brown notebooks, one with a watery stain on the front, the other with a miniature golden galleon in full sail. Some hand-drawn maps that should have 'X' marking the buried treasure and blue edges around yellow islands but are just faded ink squiggles and patterns I don't understand. I pick one of them up and it crackles, so I put it down again in case it falls apart like a winter leaf. It's just old, tatty rubbish.

Mimi flips through the first notebook and her eyes get misty and happy all at the same time. She presses the book flat so the pages spread out like butterfly wings, points to pencil drawings of fossils with careful black letters underneath each one. I trace them with one finger:

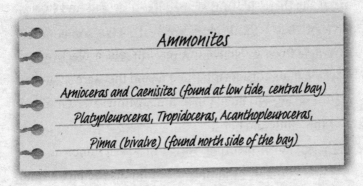

Ammonites

Amioceras and Caenisites (found at low tide, central bay)

Platypleuroceras, Tropidoceras, Acanthopleuroceras,

Pinna (bivalve) (found north side of the bay)

'A stickler, Grandad Ted,' she says. 'Took such care with everything he did. Wanted it right. Which is why,' she says, lifting out the galleon notebook, 'what you'll find in here – and here –' she runs a finger over the leaf-thin maps, gentle as a breeze – 'should NOT be sneezed at.' She smiles a wide smile, says, 'I've always thought someone should look into this, and I think you might be just the one to do it, Jonah. If you'd like to . . .'

I stare at it all, wonder what I'm supposed to be seeing and whether the dusty tickle in my nose that might become a sneeze any minute is allowed. I hold my breath, in case it's not. I shrug, shake my head. 'What . . .?' is all I manage without breathing. And because her eyes are stars and I'm scared I'll snuff out the sparkle.

Mimi reaches underneath the maps and holds out a closed fist. When she opens it, a dull chunk of silvery metal sits there. It's tiny, shaped like a slice of pizza for an elf (not that I think elves are real). Like someone cut a triangle from an old coin. 'A piece of coin?' I say. And the words fall over each other as I let my breath go, making me sound excited too. 'A very old one . . .'

Mimi nods and her stars shine brighter. 'Exactly, Jonah,' she says. 'You've heard of "pieces of eight", haven't you?'

I nod. 'Pirates,' I mumble. *Rio*, I think, and I try to hold up a smile, keep staring at the pizza coin.

'Well, that's what this is,' Mimi says, pressing it into my palm where the key had nestled. 'A piece of an eight-sided coin. An eighteenth-century Spanish eight reale. Sometimes they cut them into eight actual pieces, like this, for trading. Smugglers coming in on Spanish ships probably had pockets full of them.' She taps the notebook. 'According to Grandad.'

She flips through the bundles of maps, gentle as a breeze. Chooses one, opens it up on the desktop and smooths it with her arm. 'This is a rare find, Jonah,' she says, her words jumping like Rio's used to do when he wanted his favourite story. 'And here,' she goes on, 'is where Grandad found that coin. In a cave. Right –' her finger hovers over a swirl of dark ink on the map, lands – 'right about here!'

She sits back, arms folded across her chest, as if she's about to tell me I've won the lottery with my pound ticket. 'The legendary forgotten smugglers' booty and shipwrecked treasures have stayed undiscovered, all this time,' she announces. 'Just waiting to be found. Grandad researched it all carefully before he got sick. And he was *so* sure of his ideas . . .'

She leans across me, brings down a silver photo frame from Grandad's desk, blows dust from it. (Or sand, maybe, because that gets everywhere.) 'Here he is, bless him.'

An old man smiles from behind the glass. His hair is frosted but his skin is dark like Lois's. Like mine. It's creased and crinkled like tree bark. He has Mimi's star-sparkle eyes and a gap between his front teeth.

It's a nice face and not one that might hide lies. But it's a proper grandad face too – like in adverts for sweets and Christmas on the telly. Those kind of grandads weave stories that make children's faces into stars too, so maybe he stitched together his maps and his notes and his pizza coin into a story for Mimi and Lois, and it grew and grew until he believed it himself. Or maybe he just got muddled up like old Mr Amos next door to our old flat, who sometimes thought I was his son.

Or MAYBE it IS true, and no one believed him. Jo said that happens to old people a lot, even though they've been here longest; learned the most.

'He looks nice,' I tell Mimi.

Her smile spreads. She presses his picture to her chest. 'He was,' she says. 'Special.' She sets the photo frame back on the desk – gentle-soft, as if she's settling her grandad in his chair. 'It's all here,' she says, 'in these books and maps, Jonah. If someone would just take it seriously and follow up the trail. I wish they would. For Grandad.' She sighs. 'I've tried myself over the years but got nowhere.'

The kitchen clock chimes, breaking the spell. 'Goodness. Bedtime, I think,' Mimi says. 'You must be exhausted after the day you've had. I know I am!' She shuffles everything back together, locks the box and clears a space for it beside Grandad's picture on the desk. 'I'll leave it here for a bit – in case you'd like to look through properly. You know where the key stays. I know you'll be careful with it.' And she drops it inside the secret drawer.

'Thank you, Mimi,' I say, and a warm wave spreads in my chest because she's trusting *me* – Bad-Luck Jonah – with secrets and precious, easy-to-lose things.

I lie in bed, pull the bobbly eiderdown up to my chin. My head is fizzing like Rio's birthday lemonade. For once

I'm not worrying about the hiss of the sea behind the window. I'm thinking, what if Grandad Ted *was* right and his maps and loopy notes could lead to smugglers' spoils? What might be there, waiting to be found? Gold coins tumble behind my eyes. Gemstones flash blue, red and green between bronze goblets. Muskets with silver handles and amber bottles of bitter whisky. If someone could find them. If *I* could find them, there'd be a massive reward and I'd be intrepid and famous and just the kind of big brother that Rio needs. No one could call me Bad-Luck Jonah any more. I'd be rich. I could buy me and Rio a house. An actual *house* of our own that no one could take away from us. I'd be on the telly and Mam would see me – and she'd come back. For sure.

I *have* to find that stash.

I have a new plan. A Seriously Good Plan. At last.

All I need to do now is work my way through Grandad's box, work out where to find his smugglers' cave. The fizzing turns to thunder in my ears. The caves are in the bay. In the cliff face. Carved out by the sea, which can roar back inside them, reclaim them, any time it wants.

I pull the eiderdown right over my face and Jonah the Intrepid, Jonah the Brave, disappears.

CHAPTER 17

In the morning, two more pieces of a plan to find the smugglers' treasure click into place, as if someone laid them out on my pillow like a Christmas present. I run downstairs to have another look at Grandad Ted's box and my feet are fast like the fox. But when they hit the last step of the stairs, Mimi calls me to the kitchen. I can smell salty bacon and toast, which means she's got breakfast on the table even though I'm up ages earlier than usual and I don't know how she's done that.

Her head appears round the kitchen door. 'Come and sit down, love,' Mimi says. 'Someone to see you . . .' and my heart does a little hop-skip because maybe Mam has come back, which is stupid because she doesn't even know where I am.

It's Not-Nadia. The bacon was for her. She's sitting at the table and the cat that hates me is sitting on her lap with a narrow stare that says, 'See, you're the only one I don't like. You're the problem.'

My hop-skip heart drops like a stone into my stomach. This is it. The bit where Not-Nadia blasts me for running off yesterday, tells me she's moving me somewhere else. Somewhere further away from Rio and with locked doors and an electronic eye that watches me from the wall the whole time, so I'll never be able to get to Rio. Won't even get to *start* my search for the smugglers' stash.

I stay in the doorway, in case I need to escape. And because my legs have stopped working.

'Hello, Jonah,' Not-Nadia says through a mouthful of bacon (which is bad manners, especially for a grown-up). She swallows it down, dabs her mouth with a piece of kitchen roll, leaves a purplish lipstick kiss on it. 'Sorry to arrive so early, but I wanted us to have plenty of time this morning . . .'

She's saying something else, but it's like someone's got their hands over my ears and the words are far away.

Mimi pulls out a chair for me, sets down a mug. Steam curls from it, reaches towards me. Mimi smiles. 'It's OK, Jonah, Nadia and I have talked about last night. You're not in trouble.'

She comes across, takes one of my hands in hers. Her skin is rough and warm and feels like caring, but she can't help me, because social workers are in charge.

And anyway, looking after kids is just her job and the caring might not be real.

I pull my hand away, but I do go and sit down because my legs might give out any minute. No way am I letting Not-Nadia see I'm scared. I shift my chair back from the table, back from Not-Nadia, and it screams on the tiles, just like before, which is probably an omen. I wrap my hands around the warm mug, watch Not-Nadia's face over the rim. Some of her trapped-down hair has come loose. Wisps of grey hair stick up like wire on both sides of her head. She looks like a beetle. Or an alien.

What's coming, then? Why is she here?

'I understand how difficult things feel just now, Jonah,' she says. Which she definitely doesn't, unless someone's stolen her little brother, moved her around like a piece of furniture and hidden her somewhere her mam will never find her. 'But I do need you to promise me that you'll not run off like that again,' she goes on. 'It's my job to keep you safe, OK? You need to talk to Mimi – or to me – and it's fine to be angry at us. Just no putting yourself in danger like that.'

'OK,' I say, and I promise, which feels bad because I don't mean it. But 'not bad' as well. Because grown-ups break promises all the time and because I won't be running off like that next time. I'll be going somewhere else . . . on a mission to help my brother.

Not-Nadia nods and says 'good' and that she's 'just on the end of the phone' and to 'tell Mimi if you need her'. I nod too, though there's no chance of me needing her. Ever.

She tells me Rio and I can meet again next week – Tuesday, if I'd like that – because it might help. She rambles on about other stuff too – something about new parents again, something about a 'Review Meeting' after that. My ears close over. All I can hear is that I'm seeing my brother again in ONE WEEK. And this time we're going to Scarborough and not a stupid swing park near Mimi's town. Scarborough town is where Jo lives. With Rio. So no new parents yet.

And this time when I tell Rio I have a plan to keep him with me, I won't be lying or making ice-puddle promises.

CHAPTER 18

On Tuesday, I'm dressed in a flash, in a bright green sweatshirt that Mimi bought me. I hate it because it shouts too loud and I can't hide in it, but Rio will love it because it's green like Shrek in his favourite Disney cartoon. Before we leave, Mimi brings a long cardboard box into my bedroom. There's a picture on the top of a boy punching a red ball on a long stick. He's wearing boxing gloves and everything, and he looks pleased with himself for some reason.

'I don't think I like boxing,' I say, hoping that's not too rude.

'No, me neither,' Mimi says. 'All that punching. But this is different, it's a "feelings punchbag", just for you. A place to bash it out safely if feelings are too big for words and too heavy to keep inside. We'll set it up as soon as we're back. OK?'

'OK,' I say, because if that helps me get back with Rio, bring it on. But as we get in her triple-bubble car, my stomach flips and twists and can't decide how to be.

They're letting me see Rio. Which is a good thing. But Mimi thinks I'll need that punchbag when we get back. Why?

Does she know something I don't?

Not-Nadia's car rumbles on until the sea is quiet, and the streets straighten out and the houses don't push and shove against each other like lines of kids when the school dinner bell goes. There are fields and still skies. Tall chimneys, then the wide green verges that mean we're getting close to Jo's house. To Rio.

But the car swings left, down a road with lines of traffic and massive shops, and I don't know where we are any more.

'This is the wrong way,' I say, but Not-Nadia smiles her social worker's painted-on smile in the driver's mirror. She flicks her indicator, turns into a wide car park. 'We thought it would be nice for you boys to meet at the new play centre,' she announces. 'Where there's plenty of space.'

My heart ticks time with the indicator. There it is. The second thing they didn't tell me. First Rio and I can't have the same social worker any more. Now I'm not allowed at Jo's any more. No running up to Rio's room to check if he really is OK. No chance to snuggle up on his dinosaur duvet and tell him stories, tell him about my plan where no grown-up ears are listening.

No being just Jonah and Rio.

The ticking stops. The car slides into an empty space, stops. It feels like my heart is about to stop too.

'WHY?' I say and the word explodes in the still, silent car, louder than I meant it to be. 'Why can't we be at Jo's? Like before?'

Not-Nadia turns in her seat. Her mouth opens, but I don't hear her answer because Mimi squeezes my hand, points out through the window.

Nadia's danger-red car. Nadia locking her briefcase in the boot.

Rio. In his fox-ear bobble hat and a new red duffle coat that comes past his knees. Hand in hand with Jo, his helter-skelter hop-skipping feet hurrying across the tarmac.

I'm out of the car in a flash and *my* feet are helter-skelter too.

CHAPTER 19

It's Rio but *not* Rio this time too. He's sitting still at the table, for one thing. Not gulping down his strawberry milkshake and spilling it down his chin, for another. He's just looking at me like he's not sure I'm real. I feel sick, look around me . . .

'So what have you been up to in the bay, Jonah?' Jo says with her 'it's all right, Rio' hand on his. 'Found some good fossils, have you?' She pushes his glass a bit closer to him. 'Your favourite,' she says.

Rio slumps back in his chair, bottom lip out. 'Not,' he says, and folds his arms across his chest. His helter-skelter feet swing out, catch Jo on the leg, make her jump. But she keeps her hand where it is.

'How about the soft play area, boys,' Nadia says, pointing. 'Looks fun, eh?'

I'm too old for soft play and she should know that, but Rio is already sliding down from his seat. There are bright squidgy blocks for jumping, a shiny slide, and rainbow ball pit to land in. A Rio place, for sure. One where we can both hide from grown-ups. One where Rio might come out from behind his eyes.

He steps from one block to another. Still not Rio. Then he stops, starts fiddling with the toggles on his coat. 'Hot,' he says, and he lets me help him take it off.

'A Paddington coat,' I say. I feel inside the pockets. 'Got any marmalade sandwiches in here? I'm starving.'

There's a flash of Rio colours. His eyes search my face and a tiny hiccough-laugh escapes before he can stop it. 'Silly,' he says.

He goes towards the slide, climbs in his Rio one-foot-at-a-time way to the top, stops. 'Watch me,' he calls, and whizzes down headfirst into the ball pit. The laugh bursts through in full colours as he digs his way free, stands wobbling, knee-high in jostling balls.

I can feel Nadia's social-worker hawk eyes and ears straining, so I go down the slide too, join Rio in the balls, sending an explosion of rainbow colours in the air because I'm almost eleven and h e a v y. Rio squeals, throws himself on his back among them, right next to me. We spread our arms and legs, try to make plastic snow-angel shapes, but the balls tumble over us like they're alive.

Rio's cheeks are robin red. His fox-ear hat has fallen off.

He digs for it, plonks it on my head, grins. He asks about the fox, wants to know all about her, all over again. I describe her fire-red coat and black 'boots', her golden marble eyes, and his eyes are marbles again too. I tell him she lives in a cave and it might even have been used by smugglers – or pirates. That some people want to chase and catch her, but that I'm going to help her stay free so she can find her family again. That he and I are going to be together again too, whatever Nadia says.

He sits up suddenly, poker-straight, looks away, and throws balls out over the barrier.

'Keep the balls inside the pit, please,' Jo shouts. Rio just throws more, and harder.

'Why you keep staying away, Jonah?' he asks, and his wobble-words are steel spikes right between my ribs.

'All right there, boys?' Not-Nadia calls. I don't reply because she knows the answer. And because there's a dagger in my heart and she and her social-worker friends put it there. I HATE, HATE, HATE THEM.

'Just a couple more minutes, Jonah,' she calls. 'Then come and have your drinks, and a chat, please. We have brownies too, if anyone's interested.'

I glance over at the table. She, Mimi and Jo lean in over their coffee cups, agreeing their plans no doubt, deciding things they won't tell me until it's too late.

Well, I have a plan of my own. Thanks to Grandad Ted.

I turn my back to them all, put my arm around Rio. I tell him as much as I dare of my own plan, make it sound like a story in case he gives it away because he's only four. No one should make him keep secrets, so I don't do that. But I think he knows, because he turns back to me, nods his head like it's too heavy for his shoulders. His marble eyes are too old for his face.

I wait for him to ask for another pinky-promise, but he doesn't. The dagger shifts and jabs because maybe he's given up on those too.

'Want to see our red fox, Jonah,' he says. His hand slides into mine, fingers sticky, as always.

'You will,' I say. 'Soon.'

One teardrop escapes, zigzags down to his chin. Words pour out too. 'You gots to come for me quick, though, Jonah,' he says. ''Cos the daddies that bought me my Paddington coat, they said I got to live at their house soon . . . and they took me to see it, an' it's got grass and a tramp-lene an' a dog with a pink nose an' sweets in a jar even when it's not my birthday.' He wipes his sleeve across his face, stares down at his shoes. 'I didn't mean to go there, Jonah.'

So that's it. The reason for 'bringing forward' another visit with Rio. The 'possible forever family' Mimi told me about: they're already stealing my brother.

My fists tighten. Rio wriggles his fingers away, his face crumpling like paper. 'Stupid coat,' he mumbles. 'Don't want it anyway.'

And my heart is crumpling too because he thinks I'm angry with him for that visit, for wearing a warm coat that's just right for him. I think of the shiver-thin jumble-sale coats Mam got us; Rio's 'cold bones' next to me on our draughty mattress, and I tell him that his new duffle is the best coat I've ever seen, and if I had it, I'd definitely wear it all the time.

'You've got to keep warm,' I say, 'so you can grow stronger and bigger, ready for our adventures together.'

He hesitates, then shrugs it back on, makes me help him do it right up to the neck, pulls up the hood over his fox-ear hat. He looks smaller than ever, peering out like a wary baby bird from the too-big coat, and my heart bursts because he's brave as a lion, and he believes in me.

Jo takes one look at my storm-face and leads Rio to the toilet even though he says he doesn't need to go. Not-Nadia says, 'Come and sit down a minute, Jonah.'

But no way am I doing anything *she* says now. She and

Mimi are explaining again, passing words across the table like they're cards in a game. This time, they get through my shield . . .

'. . . for the best – like we said . . .'

'Rio's needs . . . the chance of two parents . . .'

'. . . so young . . . how much you love him . . .'

'They're dying to meet you . . . lovely couple . . . Phil and Amos . . .'

'Brothers "Together Apart" . . . still what you both want . . . if that's the right thing, as you grow . . .'

'. . . remember, Jonah? Always be Rio's brother . . .'

I can't look at her. I stare down at Mimi's cold coffee, at the skin stretching across the top. Pale. Dead skin. I'm soldier-stiff, like the skin is stretching over my body, around my heart too. I'm shrivelling inside it. A Jonah fossil. Trapped.

Rio is being pulled away from me RIGHT NOW – from his *real* family, and the only rescue plan I have depends on an old man's scribbles and searching for a smugglers' stash that might not even exist.

In caves licked by the sea . . .

If ever I needed to be Jonah the Best Big Brother, Jonah the Brave, Jonah the LUCKY, it's now. I need to find that smugglers' stash. And quickly.

'When?' I say, with someone else's voice. 'When are you giving him away?'

They fire more of their arrow words, but they bounce off my Jonah shield, can't get inside.

The only bit I hear is 'four weeks if things go well – maybe less' and the number scratches at my heart like a flint. Flames spark like panic.

It's OK. It's OK. Breathe. In, out. In, out . . .

You can do this, Jonah. YOU CAN.

I picture Freddie, wandering by the sea like it's his friend; think of the young fox, sheltering in her cave, sheltering from the surging storms and the searching eyes of those who wish her harm. Animals *know* things, don't they? She wouldn't hide out in the caves if waves could find her, sweep her away. Would she?

FOUR weeks to save Rio. Less.

I'm going caving.

Grandad Ted, Freddie – and the fox – they'd better be right. They're all I've got.

CHAPTER 20

I don't speak at all in the car. I watch buildings, chimneys and trees shift backwards as we rewind our drive, and it's like my day is unravelling in front of my eyes. Just like my life.

If I close my eyes, all I can see is Mam's stupid sand heart and the sea erasing our three names, one by one. I clench my fists so hard that the knucklebones are white through the skin. I think suddenly of our first-ever foster carers, Damon and Will. Of their giant, scaredy-cat dog, Milo, who became a snarling wolf if they brought him knucklebones from the butcher's; long white teeth bared if you as much as looked at that bone. Because underneath his daft, droopy ears and clumsy feet, he was a wild wolf and just protecting what he needed to stay alive.

I glare at the back of Not-Nadia's head and wildness is in me too. Mimi is looking at me. Perhaps she can see my long sharp teeth and the fire fizzing in my chest.

'You OK, pet?' she asks, and her voice tries to slide

under my armour, make fire into tears. I won't let it in. 'You just bash it all out on the punchbag when we get home, sweetheart,' she whispers. 'That'll be a start anyway. Then we can talk or not talk. Whatever you need.'

She thinks I'm going to sit back and let this happen, just sit there and whimper and lick my wounds like a whipped puppy. She's wrong.

I picture the punchbag. It's round head and thin, wobbly leg. Could PUNCH, PUNCH, PUNCH until the wildness in me kills it, shreds its red skin and soft innards all over Mimi's carpet. *Then* they'd see. Stop thinking they can push me around. Ignore me. Take everything I need to stay alive . . .

I shake my head. 'No stupid punchbag,' I hiss.

I am Milo with his bone.

I am the fox who runs alone and free and fierce.

Wild. Brave.

Jonah the Brave.

And *no one* is stealing my brother.

We don't go straight home, after all. Maybe Mimi can feel the heat building in me like steam in a kettle; too hot, too wild for the stupid punchbag in my room, because she asks Not-Nadia to drop us at the seafront 'for a bit of fresh air'. This time, my heart doesn't beat danger, because

129

danger is already here and it's not the sea this time.

'We'll not go far, Jonah,' Mimi says. 'Tide's coming in and the waves are whipping up a bit. Just sometimes it helps to have space around us for a bit, when things feel too heavy.'

I stuff my hands in my pockets, keep my head down. What does she know about anything? But Mimi might think I'm scared so I look up, stare at the churning waves and dark clouds rolling in like bombers, and it's like someone's painted the inside of me on to the outside, like maybe the sea and sky and wind are me. I run, although I don't know why, and I *am* the wind, tearing through the world, ripping leaves from the trees, tiles from roofs, hats from heads, snapping great branches and hurling them into the road like broken fingers, just because I can . . .

Cold grips my ankles like chains in a dungeon. Cold water. I'm at the shoreline.

The sea has caught me. My heart is a trapped bird banging around in my chest and it's hard to breathe.

I refill my lungs with salty air. I stare out across the ocean. It stares back, vast, bullet-grey and glassy. 'I HATE YOU, I HATE YOU, I HATE YOU,' I yell, and the wind whips my words away; silences them. The waves just keep rolling in, sweeping over my shoes like I'm in the way.

Like I'm nothing.

I want to turn and run. I don't. I am thunder.

I glance over my shoulder for Mimi. She's plodding over the sand towards me, but still out of earshot with the roar of waves and wind.

I stretch up tall. Face the sea. It throws its net over my cheeks, spits sand in my eyes.

I draw in a huge breath.

'I'm not scared of you,' I shout. 'You can't stop me getting my brother back.'

Maybe it's love that makes you brave.

Then the pull of the sea is beneath me, dragging my feet down into the wet sand and my teeth are chattering. I turn and run back up the beach.

Mimi is sitting on a rock, watching me, her black hair hanging like soaked string on to her shoulders. 'Wind took my hat,' she says. 'Never liked that one anyway.' She smiles, pulls up my coat collar and hood. This time, I don't pull away.

'Sorry,' I say. 'For – you know – running . . . I couldn't . . .'

'No,' Mimi says. 'No need for sorry, pet. Like I said, better to get things out. Running's good for that. You were always in sight, so that's what matters. Besides,' she adds, reaching into her pocket, 'look what I found, right beside this rock as if someone left it here specially for us. How lucky is that?' She opens up her hand.

'An ammonite,' I say.

And Mimi's right; it's perfect. Every line of the long-dead creature clear as if sketched in ink. Best I've ever seen. I slide it carefully into my pocket. It's an omen. And this time it's a good one.

'Best be getting back,' Mimi says, and as we stand a movement in the cliff face catches my eye. I'm being watched. I can feel it.

The cliff face here is patched grey and red, with glimpses of woodland along the top. There's a dark space: a large hole, maybe. No, a small cave, rounded like a Hobbit hole. Is someone – some*thing* – in there?

I creep forward, peer into the darkness. A scuffle. A sweet-strong scent in the musty air.

The fox. It's her. I know it.

The snow-white patches on her face and chest dance like disconnected puppets in the darkness of the Hobbit hole. Above them, her eyes gleam golden. This time, she speaks: a tiny 'yip' and I think she might come forward again. But Mimi is there at my shoulder, and she vanishes like a trick of the light.

'Is this one of them?' I ask. 'A smugglers' cave?'

My voice bounces inside the black space, comes back to me.

Mimi nods. 'Could well be. You ran further than you think, lad. So did I! We're in Boggle Hole – lovely little cove, bit out of the way so it's usually quiet, even in the summer. There are a fair few caves like that one there – small ones, carved out by the tide in that particular circular shape you can see.'

'Boggle?' I say, rolling the word around my mouth.

Mimi laughs. 'Gets its name from the goblins believed to have haunted the caves. Mischievous little imps they were. Folk said they could turn milk sour just by looking at it. But they used to bring their sick children to the hob holes, because they believed the little rascals also had magical healing powers.'

If only they were real, I think. *I could use some magical powers right now*. But I store Mimi's story away to tell Rio.

Walking takes ages because I am empty, my legs hollowed out like the driftwood scattered across the beach. But I don't mind. My mind is whirring.

I saw the name Boggle Hole on Grandad Ted's map. And Mimi says this was smugglers' territory. So maybe I've stumbled one step closer to finding the smugglers' hidden stash. And the fox being there – again – in Boggle Hole – *in a hob hole* – that *has* to mean something too.

She *was* there. She was real. Not like that time in my dream. I'm sure of it.

And she's telling me I'm on the right track. I'm sure of that too.

CHAPTER 21

Back at the cottage, I wait for another of Mimi's 'talks' but it doesn't come. Instead it's another hot bath, toasted sandwiches with dripping strings of cheese that stick to my cheeks, and chocolate muffins fresh from the oven.

Worry about Rio sits like a stone next to the food. But there's a spark of excitement beside it because I stared in the face of the sea and it didn't swallow me, and because just maybe, with the fox to help me, I can be Jonah the Brave and find that treasure. My hands itch to get out Grandad's maps and search for Boggle Hole. My legs jiggle because there's not much time.

Mimi produces a long wooden pencil box crammed with crayons and a roll of pristine white paper, because 'drawing is calming, isn't it?' And she fetches the ammonite from my pocket too, places it next to me without another word.

I'm not sure how she knows about drawing – maybe Nadia wrote it in one of those forms she gave her when I moved in. The ones I was supposed to write on, too;

to tell Mimi all about myself so it would be easier to settle in. I didn't want to. Settle in.

Right now, I'm sort of glad she knows this bit about me. It feels nice that she remembered.

I don't want to disappoint her, so I smile like I'm *really* pleased. I choose a dark brown crayon because it has a nice sharp point. My fingers feel fizzy, but they start to form the curls and swirls of the ancient sleeping creature and my mind follows so there's no room for worries or thoughts that stab between my ribs. That's another reason I like fossils, really. They have clear lines and shapes that stay in my head and come out on to paper. Not like the maths puzzles and spelling words at school that don't make any sense at all.

The sketch is one of my best. Mimi smiles and nods, says I'm talented, which is what Jo said too. I'm not sure if it's true, but I feel proud.

Mimi gives me a see-through folder to keep it clean, a big brown envelope and a first-class stamp so the post will get it to Rio quickly. That's definitely kind. There's a lump in my throat like when you swallow a piece of cheese too soon. But then I think, maybe it's got to get there quickly because Rio is leaving even sooner than they said, and the lump is a stone that wants to choke me.

Grandad Ted's box calls to me from under the stairs. I need to get started on those maps and notes. There's no time to lose.

I sneak a torch from the dresser drawer, curl under my duvet, wait for the thud of Mimi's bedtime feet on the creaky wooden stairs, the velvet patter of the cat who always follows her to bed, the sliver of light around my door as she peers in to check that I've settled to sleep. I wait some more, watch the moon shadows slide higher on my bedroom walls.

Mimi's soft snores drift though my wall. I creep downstairs, keeping my feet to the edge of the staircase to avoid the creaks. My heart beats double time until I'm back in my room with Grandad Ted's box. I unfold his three maps, lay them on the carpet, sweep the torchlight across them. They are crackle-crisp with age under my hand and even though I'm feather-soft, the first one I smooth out starts to split along the fold lines. I bite my lip. Will Mimi notice? She asked me to be careful . . .

I move the torchlight closer.

The ink is faded, everything sketched there now

a muddy grey. There's a smudged heading in looped handwriting . . . underneath it, faded brown galleons with masts and rigging, smaller boats – fishing vessels – sail on squiggly-line seas. Others are drawn half submerged close to wavy coastlines or wedged into tiny coves, hulls sticking out of the water like the snouts of great sea mammals. Some of the vessels have names and dates underneath:

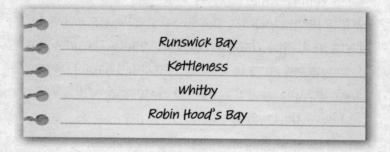

S.S. Rosa (sank 1930)

Sarb; S.S. (1944)

Wolfhound

The Jeanne (Belgian, 1932)

The Admiral Von Trump (1976)

There are place names too, some still readable:

Runswick Bay

Kettleness

Whitby

Robin Hood's Bay

No Boggle Hole. And only one of the wrecks seems to be in the bay itself. But Grandad has made notes at the bottom of the page:

North Yorks/Whitby coastline. Treacherous ...
a notorious destroyer of shipping. Average of
two shipwrecks a week since 1500. In 1869, the
100-mile stretch of coast between Spurn Head
and Teesmouth accounted for 838 ships — more
than two a day. (? And smugglers' craft —
unaccounted for?)
Folk living in cottages along these shores
will probably be sleeping under the timbers of
a sailing-era shipwreck!

I think of the thick, curved beam that arches over Mimi's staircase. I hear the creak and cracking of storm-beaten timbers, the screams of sailors and fishermen thrown into the swirling seas, sucked gasping for air into its depths. I shiver from head to toe. They've sent me to live with the spoils of a killer sea right over my head. Good job I've found a bit of Jonah the Brave.

I take a deep breath, look again at the map. No caves marked on it, nothing about a smugglers' hideout or route.

Just a terrible reminder of the power of the sea that will be lying in wait for me when I start exploring the bay for real.

My hand shivers as I unfold the second map. It's even more fragile than the first; grubbier too, like Grandad Ted handled it more often. I picture him bent over it by candlelight (not sure why the candles, but that's my picture), pen and magnifying glass in hand, brow furrowed under his crinkle-curled head.

My mind is jumping like it always does when I try to concentrate on something important. Grandad Ted's pale wavy sketches and curved letters jump too, and I can't make them join together. Some areas are too smudged to make out anyway, and there's a deep blue stain on one corner, like he knocked over an inkpot.

I don't know what I'm looking at. My eyes are full of sleep, and I need better light if I'm to make sense of anything in front of me.

Then I spot it, faded and split into two across one of the folds:

BOGGLE HOLE

Underneath the letters, a small sweep of coastline and, shaded in traces of grey and red ink, what must be cliff face. Grandad's attempts at spiky treetops run above it, just a hint of green in the cracks of the tissue-thin paper.

There's another footnote, too in wobbly capitals:

SEE BOGGLE HOLE IN DETAIL/HOB HOLE PLAN (MAP 4)

My mind is whirring now. My heart hop-skipping like Rio's happy feet.

I was right. Boggle Hole is highlighted.

'Meticulous/systematic, careful', that's what Mimi called Grandad Ted. I whisper the words into the darkness. They stretch my mouth and make him feel closer. This research was his proudest work. So why the capital letters on this map? Why the wobble and the spilled ink?

He was excited about something, I know he was. Something in Boggle Hole.

I snatch up the last of the maps. Was the answer here? Was this a map of the caves – the hob holes – of the smugglers' trail leading to the mysterious hidden stash? Must be!

I didn't see any other maps in the box.

The paper shakes like an excited bird. I'm terrified it might fall apart. I lean in, my torch just an inch away from the paper . . .

No number. Just the heading:

Jet mining . . . North Yorks coastline.

Nothing about hob holes, smugglers or Boggle Hole.

It's not the right map.

I grab Grandad Ted's box. Map 4 has to be here. I must have mis-read it somehow.

No. Just his battered notebook, the fossil, the pizza-shaped 'piece of eight' and some old wire glasses in a blue case.

No more maps.

My heart sinks like a broken boat. That's it? A dead end?

Could Grandad have hidden the fourth map somewhere else, to keep it safe? Has someone else found it already?

Or maybe he never got to draw it out. Maybe he got sick before he could.

I lift the glasses from their blue case, try them on. Everything blurs out of focus and my head feels funny. The lenses are thick like the icicles I snapped from Jo's front porch before Christmas, so me and Rio could play sword fights – until Jo said it was dangerous. I fold the glasses back into their blue nest carefully, because they're a bit of Grandad Ted and Mimi loves him.

Then there's an ice chip in my stomach because I'm no further forward at all in my plan to be with Rio again.

I start to pack everything away, flip open the notebook – although it won't be any use. It's his fossil-find record. I've seen it already.

I've got it upside down, have it open at the last page, not the first.

And there's some kind of map drawn there! More of a diagram, really, a bit like the ones we used to get in maths. Or a puzzle maze from one of Jo's mam's old-fashioned magazines.

The ink is faded here too, and Grandad's writing is tiny. Tiny, like he needed to cram all the words on this one page, or they kept tumbling out nonstop like Rio when he's had blue food colouring and he talks so fast he's like a robot gone wrong.

In this light, only two things are clear. The label at the top:

MAP 4: HOB HOLES AND TUNNELS

And right at the bottom of the page, the letters, SR, and a smudged drawing of something vaguely round in shape.

MAP FOUR. I have it!

But am I missing something? I risk turning on my bedside lamp, hold up the page to the better light.

Nothing more to see. Nothing any clearer.

SR – what does it mean? Smugglers' Route? Could that be it?

But there's nothing about a hidden stash. If it exists. Nothing to show me where to look. No arrows or crosses in excited red ink. Just a page of wandering lines, tubes, circles and dead ends that remind me of a maize maze we once went to with Mam on one of her visits. We carried flags on tall sticks so she could find us over the green hedges if we got lost. We did. And *she* didn't. Find us. Not until Rio screamed like a velociraptor because he thought we were lost forever and someone else's mam led us to the exit.

I stare at the notebook again. It's like a birthday jigsaw puzzle with pieces missing. I need more information. Need to explore the area for real, see if the map makes more sense when I'm actually on the spot.

Only there'll be no kind lady with a ponytail to rescue me if I get lost wandering in the Boggle Hole maze. Just the tide hot on my heels to make sure I never get out again if I do.

I need some help. Some way to narrow down my search. Some way to narrow down the chances of being disappeared by the sea, like Mam.

No good asking Mimi. She'd want to come with me; want to call a halt if there was anything remotely dangerous, anything that might 'break the rules for foster-kids'. She probably only showed me Grandad's stuff to distract me from worrying about Rio; never thought I'd actually go looking for the hidden stash. And anyway, if it really is dangerous in those smugglers' caves, and if things go the way they do for a Bad-Luck Jonah, Mimi might get hurt down there. I wouldn't want that . . .

Freddie!

Freddie knows the area. Freddie hangs around the beach, is used to the caves.

And he *did* say, 'See you Jonah,' like he meant it. I've got to hope he did.

Mimi wants to invite him round for tea. The stone is back in my throat. Nothing else for it. I'll have to get her to ring him, even though I've no idea how to 'have someone round for tea'. My voice might vanish the moment he rings the doorbell.

But I'll worry about that later.

I slip Grandad Ted's notebook underneath my pillow because it feels like a slice of hope to hold on to in the night. I tiptoe back past Mimi's door with the box under my arm. Mimi is still snoring like a contented cat. She told me she'll 'always hear me' if I wake, that her grandad used to say, 'she slept so lightly she'd hear a door slam in India'.

But that was before she had to run after me all the way to Boggle Hole.

I slide the box back on to the desk next to Grandad Ted's photo. His round eyes stare back at me through the glasses that hid my own just a few minutes before.

CHAPTER 22

Mimi's face lights up when I ask if Freddie can come round for tea like she suggested.

'Lovely that you've made a friend,' she says. 'Especially a smashing lad like Freddie, who goes to your new school. That'll be such a help when you start there, pet.'

I feel bad, because she thinks it's a breakthrough, that I'm settling in, but it's really a kind of lie, because I'm just building a bit more of my escape tunnel.

Mimi knows Bill, who knows Freddie's dad from the council where they work, and within ten minutes, she's dialling Freddie's home number on her ancient black telephone that has a click-click dial with holes for your finger, and a huge handset to shout into. The ringtone is loud enough for the neighbours to hear through the walls, and no one answers FOREVER.

Then suddenly Freddie's talking in my ear – his voice spilling into the hall through the massive phone receiver. Like it's a megaphone. It's a good thing it's not a video call, or he'd see my beetroot-red face when I have to say it's *me*. And I'd see his expression when he can't remember who Jonah even *is*.

He *does* remember. Or he says he does. But he can't come for tea *any* day this week because he's got to 'do stuff' for his dad. My mouth goes dry, and I'm working out how to make my voice sound like it doesn't matter, when he says, 'Meet you at the beach for a bit instead if you want. This afternoon – about three o'clock?'

I nod, which is useless on the phone, but manage to squeeze out enough words to agree to see him on the sand underneath the old coastguard 'castle'.

'I'll show you where the fox hangs out,' he adds, just as I'm about to hang up and it's loud enough that Mimi might hear, even though she's in the kitchen. 'Haven't seen her for a few days, though, so she might have moved on.'

She hasn't.

'OK. Thanks,' I whisper, wondering how anyone ever had secrets before mobile phones were invented.

Mimi says I can go, but that's because I tell her another lie, which is that we're meeting at Freddie's dad's allotment. I had to, because she'd never let me go down to the beach by myself, and certainly not anywhere near the caves. There's probably a 'rule' about that for kids in foster care.

I cross my fingers behind my back, try not to let the lie show in my eyes because it's for Rio, and maybe that makes it OK. I still feel bad, though. Because too many people have lied to *me*. It's like having bits chipped out of your bones and if they do it too much more, you might crumble into dust.

Mimi lets me borrow her laptop after breakfast. I tell her it's to find out more about Boggle Hole and the goblins, so that I can make up a story for Rio. I'm getting too good at not telling the whole truth. Maybe I'm the same as Mam.

Mimi pops upstairs to change the beds and clean the bathroom, so I switch the laptop to speak mode, with the sound down low. Today I don't have time to juggle words until they settle into some kind of order. And I don't want to miss anything important.

I do find out more about Boggle Hole. Very interesting 'more'. The robot voice tells me that many of the hob holes are above ground level, because the tides that created them there in Boggle Hole can rise especially high. That bit makes me go cold, like the sea has already drenched me. But there's more: the difficult climb to some of the hob holes meant they were favourites of smugglers on the run from customs men, 'many of whom had downed too many good pies and jugs of ale at the local hostelries'. That some hob holes led on to tightly honeycombed tunnels, bored out by the sea bit by bit since Jurassic times. There, smugglers would 'duck and dive', evading even pursuing soldiers, who anyway were 'fearful of firing off their muskets in case they triggered rockfalls and became entombed forever inside the cliff'.

I imagine the smugglers, rough beards, scowling faces, clothes wet from the churn of their oars, picture their silent glide into the bay in small rowing boats. I see them crawling on hands and knees in the tightest of tunnels, slowed by their bulging, clanking bags of contraband – stopping to tuck them away in the pitch-darkness, so they could scramble to safety in the town, returning later for their hoard.

Maybe some of them didn't make it back but were captured in daylight by lurking officials who didn't like being beaten. Some of them, I hear, ended up at the gallows.

Stories start to crawl around my head . . .

Mimi's feet clatter on the landing so I switch off the sound in case she's about to come downstairs. I scroll down the page, capture the lines of words with one fingertip. Because there it is, in black and white: the legend of the *mysterious missing smugglers' stash, believed by some to lie inside the Boggle Hole cliff face to this day, but never found, despite many seekers.'* My heart sinks again. What chance do I have of finding it, then: a townie boy whose mind is a mess of red scribbles and worry, who can't even look at the sea without wanting to run?

Mam's voice is in my head, calling from her bedroom: 'If you haven't found your PE shorts, Jonah, you have NOT looked everywhere. There's one place you haven't looked. And that's where they are. So use your own eyes instead of asking to borrow mine.'

And she was always right. About *that* anyway. They *were* always 'somewhere' in the end. And always dirty. Mam never had coins for the launderette.

Maybe Grandad Ted knew that too. Not about the shorts or Mam and the laundry money, but about there always being somewhere left to look . . .

My legs jiggle under the table, and this time it's because they're excited. This afternoon I'm hoping to get my first proper look at those hob holes and work out what I'll need if I'm to stand a chance of solving the mystery. I just need to hold my nerve and somehow persuade Freddie to come with me, without telling him why. I don't want to be that close to the sea without someone else around.

I'll feel safer still if the fox turns up. Animals sense things, so she'll know what the sea's up to before I do.

A new worry bites at my chest. Why hasn't Freddie seen her? Is she sick? Has Pest Control caught her?

No, come on Jonah. You saw her just three days ago . . .

I Google tide times for today. Columns of numbers and letters dance in front of me like hieroglyphics, won't stay still. I manage to scribble down the times for Boggle Hole just before Mimi appears, peering over a pile of laundry in her arms. I just hope I got them right.

# CHAPTER 23

My legs wobble all the way through the tilting, winding streets towards the beach. I'm wearing boots from Mimi's welly collection because 'that's what you want for a muddy allotment'. I wonder who wore them last and where they are now. They're a bit too big even with two pairs of socks and slip-slap on the pavement as I walk. I see Rio in his first-ever wellies – spotted red like 'lazybirds'. He always had them on the wrong feet, pointing outwards so he waddled like a penguin. Remembering makes me happy and sad at the same time.

It's scarier out here without Mimi's cheerful voice beside me, or her triple-bubble car between me and the wonky outside world. Even when I'm being Jonah the Brave.

I already know she'd never lose me and Rio in a stupid maze or write things that aren't true in the sand. I've known Mam all my life, and the only thing I know for sure is that you can't rely on her for anything. That she's as unpredictable as the wind off the sea.

The sun is trying to cheer me up, bouncing small diamonds off windows and parked cars and the flask of hot chocolate that Mimi gave me. It has two cups that nestle inside one another on the top so that Freddie can share. I keep looking at them because having two cups when one's not for Rio is weird. Other kids don't share stuff with me. They curl their lip and say 'no thanks, skank', like Tommy Burston when I offered him half my school sandwich because he'd left his lunch money on the bus. I picture Freddie's quiet face. It won't twist into Tommy Burston's however hard I try. Maybe Mimi's right and he does want to be my friend. Maybe.

My lies to Mimi snake at my heels. I stuff my hands in my pockets, push my chin up and hurry towards the bit where she'll see that I was being Jonah the Best Big Brother, just doing what was needed to keep my family together. The sand is soft and dry which means the tide has been out for hours. It must be miles away because it's just a wavy sea-scribble on the horizon. Good.

Freddie's a little way down the beach, bending over a kind of skinny hoover that's gliding over the sand. *He's* not wearing wellies. His feet are bare, and there's no sign of any shoes, his jeans rolled up at the bottoms. He doesn't know I'm there until I'm right in front of him and he nearly hoovers over my feet.

'All right, Jonah?' he says, lifting the 'hoover' from the sand. I nod because no one ever wants the real answer when they ask that question. He asks if I want a go with the 'hoover', which he says is a detector that can find buried metal things like coins and keys and all sorts of stuff you can make use of, or sell at the market, maybe. So that means he's searching for treasure, like me, and I'd better be careful I don't let on about Grandad Ted's idea and my own mission in case he gets there first with his 'machine'.

Anyway, how come he's so interested in things to sell when he's got a dad to buy him stuff and a house of their own and everything? Maybe he's greedy and maybe I won't like him after all.

'C'mon, I'll show you,' Freddie says. 'This way – it's best further down the beach and round the bay a bit.' He sets off towards the distant line of the sea, stepping between hundreds of tiny tunnels in the sand that he says are made by worms.

I'd rather keep close to the cliffs and head for the caves, but I follow him in my flip-flop wellies, trying not to make the sand tunnels fall in and squash any worms.

The detector is fun, I suppose. It vibrates gently in my hands like it's alive. It beeps suddenly which means it's found something, and we dig underneath it with our hands. I think maybe it's a pirate's gold earring or a silver goblet from one of the shipwrecks on Grandad Ted's map and my heart beats double time. It's not. It's just a squashed cola can. Next, we find a cap off a beer bottle. I'm probably bringing Freddie bad luck, so I hand the detector back to him.

'Never mind,' Freddie says. 'I'll try tomorrow, just after the tide's gone out.' He looks across at the horizon. 'Want to see some caves?'

I don't need asking twice. I set off towards the bend in the bay, and the shelter of the cliff face, as fast as my wellies will allow.

It's further than it seemed when I was being the wind yesterday. The sea already has a glint in its eye before we've reached any caves. And there's no sign of the fox. My stomach feels like there are tunnelling worms in there too.

Freddie is quiet, like maybe he only met up with me to be polite. He's looking at the ground all the time, so he might still be searching for treasure, but the silence makes my stomach worms wriggle more. But Jo said to remember that people might be quiet because *they're* not sure what to say. Or because they're tired or sad or a million other things that you can't see from the outside and remembering that makes me a bit braver.

'You seen the fox today?' I ask.

Freddie shakes his head. 'Nope. No sign.' He looks at me. 'If she's moved on, that'll be a good thing. Safer for her.'

I say that I know that, but my heart doesn't. Not really. Because for some reason the fox got stitched in there the first moment I saw her; stitched in with me and Rio and the success of my treasure hunt. And if she goes away, the threads might break apart and so will Rio and me. For good. I scuff at the sand with the toe of my stupid welly.

'You OK?' Freddie asks.

'Got sand in my eyes,' I say. I stick my chin forward into a wind that wasn't there two minutes ago.

His eyes are still on me. I can feel them.

'Sorry if I'm quiet,' he says. 'It's just . . . stuff. And . . . you know.' And before I can say anything he swings the detector over his shoulder, sets off running – sort of sideways like a crab. He's laughing, but the wind steals the sound before it gets to me.

I laugh too, although my heart's not in it, and side-shuffle after him.

The beach is more pebbles than sand now. My feet twist and roll in my sloppy boots, but it feels good to be running again through the wide-open space, with the ancient cliffs beside us and the wind rushing through my hair. Freddie's hair ripples like underwater seaweed behind him

The bay bends again, sharp as a dog's leg, and we're at the place where boulders and chunks and slices of stone litter the beach, as if a giant had a tantrum and threw them from the top of the cliff.

'Keep your eyes open for fossils,' Freddie says. 'Bits of the cliffs are always falling, and the sea really sweeps in and out here, washes the surface away bit by bit and that's when you find them, revealed in the middle of chunks of rock or pebbles.' He comes to life, starts jumping from one boulder to the other, closer and closer to the craggy face of the cliff, gripping on with his toes.

He disappears.

I struggle after him in my clumsy wellies, unsure whether to keep my eyes on the cliff face or the tide. My heart is a hammer in my chest.

Where *is* he?

A hand appears, waves like a pink starfish from a fold in the grey stone face of the cliff. Freddie's face and shoulders follow.

I catch my breath and clamber towards them.

Freddie's wedged in a slit in the rock. He squeezes backwards, flips on a torch he's magicked out of nowhere. 'Welcome to my cave,' he says, swinging the beam up and round behind him.

I hover, stick my head inside the gloomy space. It's rounded, lower at the back, like the two-man tent Jo's brother let Rio and me use in the garden last summer. The walls are dark – damp, like the sea lives here and just popped out for a bit. There's a musty, mouldy smell that reminds me of our old hallway. But the floor is dust-dry and there's a kind of ledge along one side: small spaces partway up the walls like mini cupboards with no door. Freddie reaches into the highest of them, brings down a half-full bottle of water and a plastic tub. He plonks himself down on the ledge, takes the lid off the box and peers inside.

'Oh,' he says. 'Thought there were more left.' He holds the box out to me.

There's a crumbly slice of flapjack inside.

'Go on,' he says.

I'm not sure what to do. It might be rude to say no when he's being kind, but taking his last biscuit might be wrong too. I think he knows, because he reaches inside and snaps the flapjack in half. I smile, take my half and I offer him Mimi's hot chocolate. His face lights up and he drinks his share so fast that his glasses steam over like frosted windows and a brown moustache grows below his nose. I try not to laugh in case that's not OK, but *he* does and for a moment his face is sunshine, almost as bright as Rio's, and our laughing joins together in the echoey cave.

Freddie hands me his torch while he cleans his glasses. I chew my flapjack, wipe sticky syrup from my fingers, look around me. The torchlight catches on something inside a thin crevice in the cave wall above his head, flickers blue, green, silver; jewel bright. For a moment I think, *treasure*, which is daft because it would never be anywhere that obvious.

I make out the side of a jar – with a glass stopper – like the ones in old-fashioned sweet shops you see on the telly. The light sweeps away. Freddie nudges me, offers me water from his bottle.

'What's that, up there?' I say, pointing.

'This week's finds,' he says. 'My best bits.'

I twist my neck, try to get a better view of the jar, but it's high up, its sides misted. 'What for?' I ask. 'Why d'you collect this stuff?'

'Tell you later, OK?' Freddie puts his glasses back on and presses the lid back on the tin – hard, like a full stop.

At the sound, there's a scuffle on the pebbles beyond the mouth of the cave, and the fox, crouching low, creeps into Freddie's cave. She stops, still low on her haunches, head slightly turned towards the exit as if unsure whether she should stay.

Freddie reaches for the torch, switches it off, and her eyes widen, headlamps in the shrouded light.

CHAPTER 24

'Wow,' Freddie whispers. 'She's never done that. Never actually come inside when I'm here. Usually, I just leave bits of food and she waits till I've left . . .'

Hairs rise like soldiers at the ready along the fox's neck and back. Has his voice scared her? For a moment, she is frozen. A fossilised fox.

She darts to the side of the cave nearest to me. Lowers her hindquarters in slow motion. She's sitting, eyes fixed on mine. I can't look away.

'Well,' Freddie whispers, this time with his hand shielding his face, muffling the sound.

The fox stretches out her neck, sniffs. A little further, inches from my fingers. Is it the flapjacks? Did her sharp nose and hollow stomach press her on, past her fear towards the scent of food? Even sweet foreign food like flapjack?

Freddie does his mind-reading thing and slides the plastic box slowly across the floor with one bare foot.

The fox's stare narrows. She shifts backwards.

'It's OK,' I tell her, making my words soft as seagrass in the wind, like Freddie did.

She tilts her head to one side. Her ears swivel. Her shoulders are still low to the ground, her legs bent like the beginnings of an escape. I prise the lid from the box: slowly, slowly. Crumbs skitter from side to side. Hardly worth the fox's efforts. But she stretches forward again, long whiskers twitching. I put the box on the floor. She moves towards it almost in one long stretch, so that her hind feet barely move. I hold my breath, feel Freddie do the same. Her pink tongue unfurls, sweeps the crumbs from the corners of the box. It curls back over her muzzle to check for morsels caught there. She slinks backwards again.

I inch my head in Freddie's direction, hoping he might have other food stashed away: some of the sandwiches he told me he sometimes brings. I raise my eyebrows in question.

Freddie mumbles a 'no, sorry.'

I should have brought something for her. Why didn't I?

She's staring at me now. She darts to the opening of the cave. Darts back again. Stares again. Freddie and I look at one another. She's back at the entrance. She circles, round and round, kicking up small stones and sand. Runs outside, back in again.

What is the matter?

It's like she's trying to tell us something. Like when I first met her.

'Maybe she wants us to follow her,' I whisper to Freddie.

'You, maybe,' he whispers back. 'She never gets close to me like that.' He shrugs. 'More likely that's just fox body language for agitated and unsure, though. She's wild, after all, not tame.'

I don't reply. She wants something. I know she does.

She's outside now, watching me, head dipped low between her shoulders, tail arrow-straight behind her. Her pointed ears are erect, tense. Wouldn't they be flat to her head if she was nervous, unsure? Like I'd read somewhere about dogs?

I crawl after her, cursing the clumsy drag-clump of my wellies on the ground. I stand, slowly. Freddie is behind me on his silent, soft feet. The fox sprints away over the pebbles, leaps on to a boulder, waits, head turned towards us. Freddie shoulders a backpack that has appeared from nowhere, like his torch.

'Coming?' I say, hoping that he is, because back in the cave, mesmerised by the fox's golden stare, I'd forgotten the sea. Just for a bit. Now I'm looking straight at it, hoping the fox isn't going in that direction.

She isn't.

She turns left, hugs the cliff face as she runs on, head sometimes turning in our direction, waiting every so often. If I could stop, I'd pinch myself. We're by the sea, following a wild fox who seems to have something to say. If it weren't for the slap of my wellies, the sharp shoot of pain in my ankle or knee as I stumble between stone and boulder, I'd assume I was dreaming the whole thing.

The cliffs blur like a fast-forward film as we run. Freddie and I are struggling for breath now, puffing like steam trains. We stop, bend, hands on our knees for a moment, and then I realise I've been here before.

We're in Boggle Hole. I'm sure we are.

Boggle Hole where the tide comes in especially high. Especially fast.

I think of the tide tables. Try to remember. Numbers swirl in my brain. I check my watch. Stare towards the horizon at a still, flat sea. Check with Freddie, my words coming out in pieces with what's left of my breath.

'We've got ages yet,' he says, and the fox is circling again, this time balanced on a boulder, like a gymnast.

We're off.

The beach changes again. Less stony, more sand islands and moss-green slabs of stone large enough to build a house on. They're slip-slide-slimy in places, sharp with embedded shells in others. The fox skips on like it's nothing, but Freddie and me slow down, pick our way, sometimes put our hands down for balance. We scramble over clusters of huge, rounded stones that look like eggs laid by something prehistoric. Freddie tells me that the speckles, grey squiggles and circles on the surface of some of them are parts of the seabed, compressed by the weight of the water across centuries. 'Awesome, the power of the ocean,' he says.

I gulp. Picture my bones, whitewashed by the sea, pressed into these rocks for seagulls to peck at. I manage a nod. Force myself to picture Rio's face instead. Manage not to turn and run back home. It's hard work staying brave.

The light changes; paints the sky in softer colours. A new breeze lifts my hair. The sky, the sea, they work together. They're in cahoots. What are they planning? My drumbeat heart is back. Jonah the Newly Brave is fading . . .

What was I thinking? For all I know, the fox is just trying to run away from us.

For all I know, the sea has lured me here. Set a trap.

I try to slow my breathing. It doesn't work. The sky, the

165

sea, the beach whirl together. It's like looking down the tin kaleidoscope Rio got in his Christmas stocking at Jo's. My ears buzz like a hundred bees just flew in there. I might be sick.

There's a tug at my sleeve. Freddie's green-grey eyes swim into focus, low light glinting off his glasses.

I blink.

'Jonah,' he says. 'Jonah? You OK?'

I nod, try to look as if it's true. I rub my eyes.

No sign of the fox.

'She's in there . . .' Freddie points towards a round hole in the cliff face, a few metres from the ground.

'A hob hole,' I say.

'Yep.' He laughs. 'Looks like she's found herself a new home.'

CHAPTER 25

We wait a bit, but she doesn't come back out. Freddie thinks we should go; that maybe she's been trying to get away from us all this time. That she won't like us getting any closer to her den, invading it with our human scent. I hesitate. I don't want to upset her. She might think she's got to move on again. And even though that might be better, before the spring visitors come to the bay, I don't want to be the one that makes her feel unsafe in her own home. Home is meant to *keep* you safe. Even if mine and Rio's never did.

And maybe I'm imagining things anyway, getting lost in a story that's only real in my own head. But I can't shake the feeling that she's not just some random wild fox made brave by the gnaw of hunger in her belly. Something is gnawing at *my* belly too. This fox is special. I know she is. She's here for a reason. And it has to do with me and Rio. It doesn't feel right to leave after she's brought us here.

'I'll just poke my head in,' I say. 'For a sec.'

Freddie nods. Hands me his torch. 'Carry it between your teeth,' he says.

It's not an easy climb, even though the hob hole must only be a couple of metres up. My feet keep slipping back, sending tiny chips of stone skittering down, making blood panic in my ears. The ledges and footholds in the rock face are fox-sized – and even a fox would struggle in a pair of oversized wellies. I nearly bite right through the plastic torch with the effort of clinging on with my fingers. I give in, go barefoot, like Freddie. I'm sure I slice through the skin on my heels with every step. Hopefully I won't get blood-poisoning.

I don't switch the torch on at first, for fear of scaring the fox. But my scrabbling feet and hard breaths must have already done that because there's no golden stare or white flash of fur in the dark shell of the cave. When I flick it into life, it picks out a scatter of small bones, ghostly white on the dusty floor. Fuzzy drifts of fur drift like dandelion clocks as a breeze sneaks around me. So our 'starving' fox has found her own meal on the winter beach – at least once anyway.

The back of the cave is low, like Freddie's own hideout. But here I make out the mouths of two – no, three – narrow tunnels leading from the 'chamber'. They look like the vessels of a heart I saw on a poster in the hospital when Mam fell over one time, and no one knew why. There's a fist around my own heart. Mam. Will I ever see her again?

Concentrate, Jonah. Come on.

The fox has disappeared. Is she lurking in one of the low tunnels at the back, terrified by the torchlight? Or maybe one of those tunnels leads on to others, and she's far away, heading for the town for a Friday fish-and-chip throwaway. I think of Grandad Ted's diagram, the criss-cross maze of interconnecting tunnels inside the Boggle Hole cliffs. But no, these are tiny, far too narrow for smugglers in their bulky seafaring clothes, bags of contraband to push and shove between them, even if they wriggled on their stomachs like sandworms.

My heart sinks like feet in sand. I'm living in fairy-tale land here. How could the fox possibly know what I'm looking for? Why would she pick the very place that holds the lost 'treasure' for her home out of all the caves along this shore? She's just a fox, doing what foxes do. Foxes do not read minds or speak to humans. Not in the real world where I'm still stupid, stupid Bad-Luck Jonah who can't even come up with a sensible plan to save his family.

Freddie calls my name. 'Coming,' I shout, and pull back sharply, banging my head. My cry of pain bounces around inside the cave, followed by the torch, which rolls out of reach.

'All right there?' Freddie calls, and I shout back that I'm fine, even though my skull is pounding and there's the pulse of an egg growing under my hair.

'Just getting the torch.' My voice bounces around my head too, making it throb even more.

Freddie calls not to worry, just leave it, but I can't because he trusted me with it, and I let it fall.

I scrabble higher, feel the scratch of sharp stone through my jeans, pull myself flat inside the cave on my stomach, like the smuggler I saw in my mind's eye. I stretch for the torch. It rolls further away, stops right at the back, at the edge of one of the tunnels. I squeeze my eyes shut so I don't have to think about where I am or whether the sea might take its chance, rush up the beach and swallow me whole like the famous Jonah's whale. I open them as my fingers find the rubber grip of the torch.

I'm staring straight into one of the tunnels, and I was right. Tiny. Even from outside, I feel the cold press of the walls around me, crushing my ribs, stealing my breath. Holding me hostage for its accomplice, the sea. I tremble. Everything in me wants to push backwards, out into the afternoon light, but as I grab the torch, fit it back between my teeth, its triangular beam catches something on the cave wall, just to the left of the tunnel's mouth.

A letter 'A', about five centimetres high, scratched white into the dark rock . . .

No. Not a letter. A triangle.

It can't be. It's just a trick of the light. A bit of shell or debris compacted by the sea as it formed the tunnel.

I shift forward, hold the torch a bit closer.

No. It's definitely a triangle. A slice-of-pizza-shaped triangle. In the centre, faded marks broken up by green stuff that cling to parts of the rock: moss, lichen or some weird mould or something. I squint at them: there's the curve of what might have been a snake. Or an 'S'. Yes. Maybe an 'S'! Its partner is too faint to make much of.

My heart is banging against my ribs like it's trying to get out.

This can't be a coincidence. Can it?

Grandad Ted's piece of eight. I see it, feel the cool weight of it in my hand. Why was it there, in his special box, along with the maps and notebooks? What if it's more than a scrap of booty dropped from a smuggler's pocket, a hint of more to be found?

What if it's a different kind of clue?

It *has* to be.

171

Not an 'X' marks the spot for buried treasure, exactly – there's nowhere right here to hide *anything* unless you've got a pneumatic drill to get through the ancient rock. And don't mind tons of stone collapsing on your head in the process. Besides, no one would hide anything this close to the beach. Too easy to find. Too easily snatched back by the tide.

But this is *something*. A piece of the jigsaw.

I swing the torch beam further inside the tunnel. Looks like it widens a bit a few metres in. And there's a fork – one tunnel going left, the other right. Of course. The 'piece of eight' IS a marker. A marker for Grandad Ted's honeycomb smugglers' trail: SF on his sketched map!

My overexcited heart slams against my chest wall.

Drops into my boots.

Grandad Ted is telling me to follow that tunnel, to crawl further into the great belly of the cliff, further away from the light; somewhere only the sea will know where to find me.

Can I really be brave enough to do *that*?

CHAPTER 26

Scratching and scrabbling behind me. Freddie's face and shoulders at the mouth of the cave, his forehead a puzzle of wrinkled worry in the swing of my torch.

'Got it,' I say, my voice a watery squeak. I edge backwards, hand Freddie his torch. I follow him down, sliding rather than climbing in my hurry to escape the tight, dark spaces that call to me. I nearly land on top of him. He brushes dust from his hair, blows on his glasses.

'Sorry, Freddie,' I say. 'I slipped.'

He just scans me with his soft green stare, shrugs his Freddie shrug, smiles. He shoulders his backpack. 'C'mon,' he says. 'This is a good time to find stuff – when the light's low on the sand. Best a bit closer to the shoreline, though.'

I look past him, shield my eyes.

The waves are definitely coming faster, higher, like they want to eat the sandy space between us and the cliffs. I take several steps back, stare at the perfect welly-shaped imprints I've made. The sand is damper. Is the sea sneaking up from underneath our feet, ready to circle round, cut us from the cliff steps?

The tide-table letters and numbers stamp around inside in my head. *High tide: 18:45.* 'Isn't the tide coming in, though?' I say, and my words are wobbly because my watch says nearly 16:40.

Freddie turns his face to the sky, tilts his head to one side, like he's listening for something. 'Another hour, I'd say. We're fine.' He walks on, eyes down.

My feet won't follow. It's like I'm held in sinking mud. Or quicksand.

How come I was brave enough to climb into the hob hole, and now I can't even walk? I'm going to have to do a whole lot better at this bravery thing if I'm going to find that hidden treasure. And there's not much more time to practise.

Freddie gets smaller by the second. A dark stain is spreading up his rolled jeans.

Suddenly being left behind is scarier than getting closer to the sea. Energy fizzes inside my wellies. I slip-slap across the sand, catch him up.

He stoops, brushes sand from a dark stone. A twitch of a smile arrives on his serious face. I bite my lip. 'I just thought, won't your dad be home soon?' I ask. My voice wobbles. 'For his tea?'

Freddie looks up at me through his seagrass fringe. He'll smell the fear in me. Everyone does. I wait for him to laugh, but he doesn't. He stretches out his hand, shows me the dark sand-dulled stone. 'Jet,' he says. 'Whitby jet. Lucky to find any at this time of year.' His smile spreads wider.

I try to look impressed because Freddie's face is telling me I should be. I've never seen anyone look so proud of a stone. He curls his fingers around it like it might try to escape and burrow back into the sand. He nods towards the cliff face. 'Some of the caves,' he says, 'the smaller ones on this coastline, they were made by people mining for this stuff. Used explosives to blast into the rock, they did. Pieces still get washed from the cliffs – usually more in the winter, though, and people come searching for it.'

My impressed look isn't getting past the worry my face is trying to hide, because he spits on his thumb, then rubs the jet stone on his sleeve. It turns darker still.

'Yep, definitely jet,' he says, pushing it nearer to my face. 'People polish it up, make jewellery and things out of it. It's beautiful.'

I nod, remember the coal-black glitter of the necklaces and rings in the gift shop window. Remember the label that said people wore them at funerals, and Queen

Victoria started that because she was sad for about a hundred years after her husband died. 'Nice,' I say, and his smile washes away because nice is a watery word and not good enough. 'Do you, then?' I say, trying to do better. 'Make things with it?'

He shakes his head. 'Not me. Atticus down the craft market. Or Maggie, the artist lady from the gift shop. They give you money for it.'

I wonder how much someone would pay for a bit of dirty black stone, how that could be worth all the time Freddie was spending searching, all the excitement in his face. His collection back in the cave. I don't ask. The explanation might take more time than we have. My stomach twists because I think Freddie does want to tell me – that this 'finding things' is important for him; tied up with something stone-heavy in his heart. I can feel it in the air, just like I could with Mam. And Rio.

He walks on and I do too, even though my feet want to run. Back down the beach, back towards the town and Mimi's crooked house, back to bed, where I can bury my head under my duvet, hide from the sea. Hide from myself: Jonah the Coward. Jonah the Failure. Jonah the Useless.

Freddie keeps his head down. He might have forgotten

I'm there. He's a magpie, swooping at any tiny glint in the sand. I keep my eyes on the space between us and the sea. It's getting smaller and smaller, foam curling along the edges like it's getting angrier and angrier too.

Freddie stops again, scuffs at the sand with his bare toes. Something green winks up at us there. 'Ah. Sea glass,' he says. He picks it up between his finger and thumb. A chunk of green glass. He blows and spits on it, rubs it on his sleeve. 'Old bottle glass,' he tells me. He holds it up and I think, *Be careful, be careful: sharp edges*.

But when I look closely, they've been smoothed by the sea and the sand, like my fossils, and there's a glimmer right in the middle, as if a diamond is hiding there, waiting to be cut out. Freddie looks round, jumps towards a pool of water held like a mirror between the flat rocks. I follow – stumbling rather than jumping. He swirls the glass in the pool, shatters the mirror into a hundred rings. He holds the glass up to the light and the secret diamond is everywhere, shooting tiny flames into the sun.

'Perfect,' I say, because that's the best word I can think of and because the diamond fire steals a bit of my breath. It must be the right word this time because Freddie smiles again. He unbuckles his 'finds' backpack and pops the chunk of green glass inside, slowly, gently, like it's as delicate as an egg.

Sea spray drops on to my cheeks: a catch-net. The hairs on my arms prickle. 'I really have got to go now,' I say. 'The tide tables said . . .' I trail off. Now he knows I checked. Now he knows I was worried. Or a nerd. Nerd is better.

Freddie looks at me. Properly this time. As if I'm one of his stones. His eyes peer into mine, clear and green as his precious sea glass. 'People round here, they lived by the sea long before tide tables and shipping forecasts and Google and stuff, Jonah.' He looks away, shoves his hands in his pockets. 'They listened to it –' He stops. His cheeks blush pink like the seed shells under our feet. 'The sea, it's got a sort of . . . music, that's all,' he says. 'And different – different "feels". In the air. Dad taught me to listen and look. *His* dad taught him. If you listen properly, learn the music, check the air, you'll know where you are with it too. You'll be safe.' His eyebrows lift above his glasses. 'It's like Dad says: "knowledge is power". It can make big things smaller.'

'Right,' I say. 'Right.' Because I don't know what else to say. Because I like Freddie, and because he saved the fox, and she led me to Grandad Ted's first clue. Because he might be reading me, as well as the sea.

Because suddenly I'm all out of 'brave'. I want to leg it up the beach, well away from a boy that trusts in 'ancient music' and 'funny feelings' around something as dangerous as the ocean. Far away from the smugglers' trail and even the call of the fox that led me there.

But somehow my legs keep moving. I keep my eyes down so Freddie thinks I'm searching too, doesn't know I'm scared. Something crunches under my boot. A shell. Like the one in Not-Nadia's room only smashed to pink smithereens – like my heart, without Rio – lying there, pressed into the sand.

I see him. His wide, watery eyes. Like he's right here with me in his too-big Paddington coat, clutching his bags of marble 'double t-easure', waiting for me to play pirates again. Here, believing in me.

'Found something?' Freddie calls, over his shoulder.

I shake my head. 'No . . . sorry.'

But I have. I've found Jonah the Brave again.

Because losing my brother – letting him down – chipping more pieces off my heart – and his – that's the scariest thing of all.

My plan is ON. I can do it. I CAN. And no ocean in the world is going to get in my way.

I plod over to Freddie. Him and his 'sea-music', they're all I've got for now. But one thing's for sure, I'm getting some sea FACTS under my belt before I head back to Boggle Cove and Grandad Ted's smugglers' trail . . .

CHAPTER 27

The sea music is louder by the time we leave: the notes swirling closer together; louder. More bass. But Freddie *was* right. We reach the slipway to town without waves licking at our ankles like we're about to be their next meal. We had plenty of time.

My telltale legs jiggle. I'm itching to get back to Mimi's and to Grandad Ted's box. To have another look at the maps and that piece of eight, now that the fox has taken me to the starting point on the treasure trail. And I want to start my sea research in case terror creeps back with the moon.

'Thanks,' Freddie says. 'For your help.'

And I wonder what I've helped him with because I didn't find anything except more twisted cans, a filthy ten pence coin, and a very dead sea snail. He cradles his bag of bits of glass and black stones as if it's a baby or something precious, and I think he's telling me something with his eyes, just like the fox does. The moment stretches but my questions fall through a hole in the middle. His phone beeps and that tells him something that makes him blink, then he's in a hurry too, walking away backwards as he slides the phone-messenger into his back pocket.

'Want to help me with some planting in the morning?' he says. 'At the allotment. Nine-ish? I'm behind with it, with all the late storms we've had, and other stuff.'

I want to say no, because tomorrow is Saturday which means his dad might be there too and he won't want me killing off all his baby plants or stepping on his prize potatoes. But I say yes. Because I told Mimi we were going to the allotment today, and if I go in the morning, that smudges the lie – sort of – and makes me feel a bit less mean.

As I walk home, the wind pushing from behind for once, I wonder about Freddie and the 'stuff' he keeps mentioning. My senses might not help me read the sea or sky, but they know when someone can't find the right words for something because it's just too big for their mouths. Or because they're afraid that saying it will make it real.

Grandad Ted and me, we're not the only ones with secrets. Freddie's hiding something too.

I check my clothes for sand before I turn into Mimi's street. I go round the back way, through Mimi's tiny pebble and pot garden, rinse the seawater stains from my wellies under the outside tap and kick them off before I go inside.

I'd like to creep through the kitchen, go upstairs and change my socks, which are filthy after my scrabble into the hob hole. The right one has a hole by the big toe and a red scratch shows on my pink skin. But Mimi's right there, at the table, chatting to her sister Lois, who this time has a rainbow sprinkle of tiny beads braided into her hair. If Rio was here, he'd want them in his hair too.

Music is playing and it's filling the kitchen with colours: hop-skip notes that make my body want to move even though it's bone tired and needing to hide the lies. There's a massive chocolate cake in the middle of the table, glistening with scarlet cherries on top, three plates and silver knives laid out next to it. I think of Rio's birthday cake, untouched, waiting for Mam who never came to help him blow out his candles. His next birthday is going to be the BEST EVER. I'll make sure of it. I have to snuff out my fears about that smugglers' trail, about the sea. Rio. He's all that matters.

'Lois has been baking, pet,' Mimi says, beaming from ear to ear. She gets up, presses a button on her phone, and the party leaves the room. 'Come and have a slice, tell us about your day.'

'It's my speciality, Jonah,' Lois says with her matching smile. 'Just for you. We been waiting for you to have the first piece. Not easy, I can tell you!'

I stare at them both, at the cake that's making my empty stomach rumble like a tractor. They're asking about my day. The one where I'm supposed to have been at the allotment. I'll never be able to do it: sit there and twist my mouth around lies and Lois's gift cake at the same time. That's where I'm not like Mam at all.

'Wow,' I say. 'Looks amazing. Thank you! But I'm desperate for the loo, *so* . . .'

I jiggle and squirm on the tiled floor, one foot crossed over the other to hide the sock issue. 'Back in a minute.' I rush to the door. 'Don't wait, though,' I call. 'Dig in.'

I thunder upstairs and into the bathroom, wash my hands. The mirror picks out sand and grit caught in my curls, guilt in my eyes. Did Mimi notice? Probably. She doesn't miss a trick.

I go to my room, flop face down on my bed, try to make the lies I need feel more like a story; I'm good at those. But you don't get to lie to yourself, and my stomach doesn't have room for cake any more. Not even Lois's speciality.

Especially not that one, made with kindness.

Did *Mam's* lies bite at her heart like this? Some of hers were BIG ones. Lying to people that you love – to your children – that must hurt your heart worse than anything. Surely.

Unless the love is a lie too.

I see the lying sand heart, the surging Whitby sea and howling wind, and in the corner of my mind, poking through like the tide just brought it: a glimpse of a half-buried, terrifying truth.

Mam disappearing. It had *nothing* to do with the sea.

She *chose* to leave us.

I've been lying to myself too.

The thought cuts deep, sharper than a shark bite. My chances of putting things right – of ever seeing her again – feel smaller than a grain of sand. My plan to find a smugglers' haul and be Rio's hero brother, nothing more than frothy sea foam. Another lie. I'm Jonah the Stupid. Jonah the Liar. Jonah the Coward, like Mam.

I curl up like an ammonite on my bed, press my knees against the ache in the middle of me, and it's like I'm already lost in the maze of smugglers' tunnels, with no idea how to get out.

CHAPTER 28

Next thing I know, the bed dips and warmth spreads along my arm. I rub my eyes. Prop myself up on one elbow. Mimi is sitting next to me, mug and plate in hand. She puts them on the bedside table.

'Sorry,' I say. 'Didn't mean to fall asleep.'

Mimi lifts a lock of hair from my forehead. For some reason it makes me feel like crying. 'Fresh air'll do that,' she says. 'Thought you might like this up here anyway.' She nods at the snack she's brought. Steam is curling from the mug, rolling over the biggest slice of cake I've ever seen.

'But Lois, she . . . It's just, I didn't feel like . . . talking.'

'Lois understands, Jonah.' Mimi's feather hand is on my arm now. I want it to stay there but snakes are biting at my heart because if she knew I was a liar, like Mam, she'd take it away. And there'd be no more cakes, just for me. I wriggle back on the bed, knees under my chin, reach for the mug as camouflage.

Maybe, I tell myself, Mimi *would* understand, because

she has Lois and I reckon they'd fight lions to stay together. But the snakes still slither and nip and wind in my stomach. No wonder Mam never wanted to eat anything.

Mimi gets up. 'You enjoy that,' she says. 'Even if it is before your dinner. I won't tell if you don't.' I smile, take a bite and nod, like it's delicious. Which it is. I tell her that Freddie wants help with putting in his carrots and stuff in the morning, because I need to say something that's true. She seems pleased. 'It's lovely, planting things, looking after them, watching them grow,' she says, and her face is starry again like she's thinking of more than just vegetables.

She'll drop me down there, she says, say hello to Freddie and his dad. She pats my leg and says how about we watch a film together – or play a game for a bit, so maybe we're fine and she doesn't suspect anything. She pops downstairs to make pizza and popcorn and a warm feeling pushes into the lost space inside me, because that's the sort of thing families do, and Mimi wants to do it with me. Then I feel bad because Rio's my family, not Mimi.

But I can't help worrying that she scans faces and reads them like Freddie reads the sky and the sea. What if she's already told Not-Nadia she can't trust me or keep me safe? Then Not-Nadia will move me somewhere else, and I'll be like Paris Johnson in my old class who got moved from foster carer to foster carer like a lost parcel and hated everyone because then it didn't hurt when she left them behind. No one will know where I've gone. Not even Rio.

My thoughts tangle and fall over one anther like there's a maze in my head too. I feel small, scared and dizzy, like I'm spinning. Suddenly I just want to be downstairs, next to Mimi who feels solid and still and safe, even if she does live in a wonky house that's sliding towards the sea. For now, anyway.

The fox comes at night again, red fire against the dark sky. Rio and I are riding on her back and my hair streams out like a lion's mane as we swoop over a black sea. Waves leap to reach us, tunnels open below us, try to suck us into their monstrous jaws. We soar above them. My arms are tight around Rio. I am his brother who will never let him fall. Rio's laughter flashes like lightning and a world beyond the sea stretches out ahead of us, bright with rainbow colours. The fox swoops low, ready to land . . .

Then she's gone. Rio's hand is in mine as we float down to earth.

AND I AM THE FOX.
I AM FIRE.
I AM JONAH THE BRAVE.

When I wake, the fire is still there, burning in my chest and I think I know why the fox came, why she follows me. She's here to show me the wild and brave inside me. To tell me I can do it; face the unknowable sea and the dark, dark tunnels and keep my brother close.

I get out of bed. Everything is the same: Mimi's soft carpet between my toes. The sneak of sea-wind in the air. My bedside lamp throwing a moon on the dark glass between my curtains – the ones with leaves dancing. But it's like I've got one foot in my room and one still in my dream world, like I haven't quite left. Like I'm not quite me.

Or maybe I just found me.

I stand. I feel taller somehow, as if my bones and my heart have stretched, grown stronger in the night. Like I've grown wilder and I don't care about Mam and her lies or the unknowable sea; like I can do ANYTHING, all by myself.

My feet won't keep still. I want to race all the way to

Boggle Hole, start digging around in that tunnel with my bare hands. I want to trap that feeling like a message in a bottle, take it out whenever Jonah the Brave threatens to crawl away. Whenever Rio needs me to hold him tight and not let go.

My brain floats back into the real world.

Slow down, Jonah. No red-scribble running. Get this right. There is no magic bottle. You need to get this right.

In the *real* world. Where Rio is out of reach.

First things first.

Sea facts, remember?

Freddie. The allotment at nine. I'll make a start before we leave . . .

I thunder down the stairs, ducking my head under the arched shipwreck beam and only realise it's not even six o'clock when Mimi emerges, bleary eyed, in the kitchen, worrying that I might be ill. Or about to do another runner, perhaps.

'What's the emergency?' she asks, and I brace myself. You wouldn't want to wake our mam early like this, and if you did, you'd hear about it, LOUD in your ears. That was still better than some other days, though. The ones where she wouldn't get out of bed even if the roof fell in.

But Mimi sets the kettle singing and pops bread in the

toaster. She's happy for me to use her laptop but it has to be right there, in the kitchen, and not up in my room like I wanted, 'because that's the rule, Jonah'. When I tell her I want to find out more about the sea, she nods and says, 'That's the way, pet, well done,' as if she knows why I need to do this, as if she's known all along that I'm scared.

She goes to Grandad Ted's desk, brings me a notebook with a soft blue cover that feels like stroking a soft animal when I run my fingers across it. The pages are empty. 'Grandad would love you to have it,' she says. 'You can note down what you discover. Writing things down can help too.'

'Thank you', I say, but I daren't look up because she's already seeing right inside me and that's through the back of my head. But it feels kind of nice that she knows. It makes the fear a tiny bit smaller too. She sits with me as I google 'Facts About the Sea'.

Images jump up in front of me: waves rearing like great horses, crashing on to towering cliffs; ships tossed like toys. There are flat mirror seas, bottle-glass green, their depths teeming with darting fish in every colour imaginable, strange alien creatures still as secrets, tangled underwater forests that look like they belong to another world, another planet. They're awesome. Beautiful. For the first time ever, I want to know more . . .

I'm going to need a lot of notebooks.

I open my first one, grip my pen and wait for the blue screen to take me to the sea.

We eat warm toast that drips butter and makes my fingers slide on the keyboard. Mimi just sets a cloth beside me and doesn't get mad. She helps me read, breaking down the words that dance and skip out of reach of my pen. She makes it feel OK, like we're discovering things together, revealing the diamonds inside a sea-tossed stone.

By the time Mimi's phone alarm says it's time to get ready for Freddie, I've captured eight of my favourite facts. The sea doesn't feel smaller yet. It's starting to feel even bigger – but in an awesome way that makes it feel kinder. Because we found out that nearly seventy per cent of the planet's surface is covered by oceans. In fact, the oceans hold over ninety-five per cent of all the water on Earth. Water is the most important thing for life. Including me.

When I go to my room to get changed, I read my notes out loud while Mimi's in the shower, her ears blocked by the surging water and ancient, singing pipes:

1. An ocean is a huge body of open water and is much bigger than a sea. A sea is a smaller part of an ocean and is usually partly surrounded by land.

Like here, in the bay.

2. The largest ocean on Earth is the Pacific Ocean. It covers about thirty per cent of the Earth's surface. Its name comes from Latin. It means 'peaceful sea'.

Which makes it a bit like my name, according to Mam anyway.

3. The sea here in Robin Hood's Bay (and in Whitby) is part of the North Sea. It is the coldest sea in the world because it stretches all the way to Norway and Denmark (which are freezing most of the time).

That doesn't sound peaceful, or friendly, or safe. But over two hundred and thirty species of fish live there, and so do seals, dolphins and whales. So it's not just a big, icy stretch of angry water thrashing about for no reason. It's friendlier than it looks. And it's kinder to whales and dolphins than humans are from what I've learned in school.

4. Oceans across the world are home to incredible creatures that are 'masters of disguise'. (Like Mam. And me.) One of them is the octopus, which can change colour, pattern, brightness and texture in seconds, to match its environment, and for protection. It can also make itself appear very large or very small.

All of which sounds very useful and quite a bit cleverer than you'd think. You shouldn't judge by appearances.

5. The longest mountain range in the world is found underwater. It stretches over 56,000 km. It's called the Mid-Oceanic Ridge.

6. The sea is home to the world's largest living structure – the Great Barrier Reef. It measures around 2,600 km, and is so big it can even be seen from the moon!

7. People have only explored about five per cent of the world's oceans. There's a lot more to be found . . .

It's like there are whole other worlds underneath the sea . . . and not just lost ships, skeleton sailors, stolen sandals and broken promises.

8. Oceans are one big mega museum. There are more amazing treasures and remnants of history in the ocean than in all of the world's museums put together.

So Freddie's right. You never know what the sea might bring back to shore.

But the sea's not going to bring back Mam. I know that now. But if that smugglers' stash exists – if I do find it and bring Rio home – then maybe, just maybe, she'll walk right back to us on her own two feet. Changed, like the octopus.

Right now, though, even with fox fire inside me, I think the chances of that happening are narrower than any tunnel on the smugglers' trail.

But you never know . . .

CHAPTER 29

In the car, Mimi hands me a blue backpack. It's got red/gold flashes on the side that make me think of the fox. The buckles are stiff because it's new, and just mine, and not from the charity shop like my old ones. There's a pocket at the front which is perfect for notebooks. And maps. Inside, there's a kind of net bag that's probably for PE kit but is filled with Mimi's 'snacks for hungry lads'. It will be good for collecting sea-treasure when I get to teach Rio about diamonds hiding in stones and stories from underwater worlds.

Today it feels like spring in the allotment. No lashing rain to smash down Freddie's fledgling plants. The sun is warm on my head and there's a birdsong band playing from somewhere inside the hedge. Freddie is already busy, turning over the soil with a silver trowel. Some of his trays are beside him, the feathered green shoots now taller, some draped over the edges like they're trying to get to the ground by themselves. Freddie's hair is hanging over his face, his hands black with earth.

We catch him by surprise, despite the clump of my wellies and Mimi's purple boots. He jumps, as if we've brought him back suddenly from somewhere else all together.

'Oh, hi, Mimi, hi, Jonah,' he says. He stands up, pushes hair from his face, leaving muddy streaks across his forehead. I see dark shadows under his sea-glass eyes. They're nothing to do with having grubby hands. I know that.

'Lovely to see you again, pet,' Mimi says. She beams. 'I've not come to get in your way, just thought I might see your dad, say hello. Busy time this, for gardeners. I expect he's here somewhere, is he?' She glances towards the half-open shed door.

Freddie shakes his head. 'He's working this morning,' he says. A black cloud wanders across his open-sky face and I know he's lying. He's not like Mam. Or the sea. He can't hide things. His eyes slide away, back to his plants. 'He'll be here later,' he says. 'I'll tell him you were asking.' He kneels back down, eases one of the tiny plants from the tray in a square clump of earth. Its tangle of thin roots dangle in the air like a family of spiders is trapped in there.

Mimi looks at me. She's seen it too, the cloud.

She always does. 'Well, if you want some extra help,' she says, 'I'm your girl. Don't let these bright red nails fool you. Lois's idea. Happy to pitch in and get my hands dirty.'

Freddie smiles, then. 'No worries,' he says. 'We'll be OK. I've brought my friend to do most of the work.'

It takes me a moment to realise that he means me, and something new sprouts in my chest too. My own smile is way too wide for sure, but Mimi's might be even wider.

She leaves us to it with the offer of a ride home when I've had enough. Freddie gets straight back to his planting. Carrots. Apparently. He shows me how to tease away excess soil from the fragile roots, leaving some of it there because it's like a piece of home to bring with them, then to settle them gently in the freshly dug hole. He scoops the earth back around the stem with his hands, presses it firmly so that the skinny seedling stands straight.

'We do them in rows,' he says. 'Spread your fingers like this, to make the right space between them, so they have room to grow. And only put them here, in this stretch of soil; not over there.' He waves at another bed, the other side of the shed. 'Soil's not right for carrots there. And Dad's potatoes are already in.' He digs another hole. 'Like this, see. So it's just right for the roots. Once we're done, we give them a good drink. OK?'

I nod, hoping that I won't mess up and let him – and the carrots – down. He hands me a trowel. 'Start another row,' he says. 'There. Look.' He shuffles and moves away a bit, to give me space too, falls silent.

A bearded man in a duffle coat and cap rumbles past, wheelbarrow piled high with what might be weeds, and brown flower heads. He nods at Freddie, rumbles on. A few minutes later, he's back, the empty wheelbarrow now squealing as it runs over the ground, like it's protesting. The man – Arthur, Freddie tells me – sits down on a bench beside a shed that badly needs painting and drinks from a steaming flask. I turn back to my work, wondering who got to decide which plants are weeds and should be ripped from the ground and tossed out of sight.

My hands are slow, clumsy. I catch myself with my tongue sticking out like Rio does when he's concentrating super hard. Freddie's done a row of ten by the time I've managed four. But they're standing tall, feeling the sun on their pale leaves for the first time and it feels good to sink my hands in the sticky earth, helping new life grow, good to move in a kind of rhythm along with Freddie. Me, I'm usually out of step with everyone. Except for Rio.

And now, maybe the fox. Who so far this morning is nowhere to be seen.

I keep glancing at Freddie. His hands are here, gentle and deft and sure. The sun glints gold in his pale hair. But the stillness has left his face and his colours are dark, shifting like a storm sky. Something is wrong. Something about his dad.

A friend would say something.

I finish my first tray. Wheelbarrow Man leaves. The only sounds are the bird musicians, a rustle of leaves and a lawn mower roaring like a distant lion from a nearby garden. I sit back on my haunches. And I do say something.

My new truths push up into my throat, like they just pushed their way up through the earth.

'Our mam,' I say, 'she left us. Me, and my brother.'

Freddie gets up, fetches a yellow watering can from the shed, moves it back and forwards across our green rows. A crystal fountain runs over the thirsty leaves, blackens the striped ground. I wonder whether he heard me. Then he's still, the last of the water running from the can over his feet, and my words keep spilling out into the space between us . . .

'She . . . she gets . . . sick, maybe. I don't know. Lost.'

I stare at the seedlings, imagine their roots, a network of tiny anchors to keep them secure and help them grow strong, grow into their 'carrot selves'. And I see it.

Mam, she never had any roots. Never found the right ground to help her grow. Like maybe she's still the baby in the yellow blanket, helpless in her basket by the cold North Sea. Still waiting for her own mam to come for her.

Words tumble out like they've been storm-washed from the stone in the middle of me. I tell Freddie how Mam came from the sea. About Rio and his bright songbird colours. About the lying sand heart and the silvery social-worker promises that won't be real. How Rio and me, we're each other's anchors; how if we can't be together, we're bits of broken boat, lost at sea inside, like Mam. How I have to save him. Save myself.

How I need to be Jonah the Brave. Like Rio deserves.

A sob explodes through my chest, and I am empty.

Freddie sits down beside me, takes off his glasses and wipes them on his jacket. 'Mud gets everywhere,' he says. He looks up at me from under his fringe. '*That's* brave,' he says. 'Saying all of that. And just being you, in the middle of it all. That's brave too.'

I wipe my nose on my sleeve. I don't have any words left, so I drag over my backpack, offer Freddie wipes for his hands, his pick of Mimi's snacks from a bundle wrapped in checked cloth.

He takes a golden cheese scone, holds it in mid-air.

'My mam went away too,' he says. 'She's from America and she went back there. I was only one, though, so . . . it's not the same.'

I wait. Stare at the red apple in my hand.

'I can see her when I want,' he says. 'Fly out there, and stuff. Video calls. She's . . . nice. But not really, like, my mam, you know?'

He looks at me for a moment and I nod, so he knows I'm really listening, which makes me feel like Nadia in her office with the miniature chairs.

'So it's just me and Dad,' he goes on. 'Always has been.' He takes a huge bite from his scone, making his cheeks puff out round as my apple, and I think maybe he's trying to trap other words behind it. He points at a leafless young tree pinned to a wooden splint. A miniscule bird is sitting there, black bead eye fixed on the newly dug soil. 'A wren,' he says, 'checking for worms. Hope she nests nearby.'

I eat a chunk of my apple, give him space, like his new plants. But then I say it.

'About your dad,' I say. 'He's *not* coming today, is he?'

Freddie swallows. Stares after the wren as she flits from branch to branch, hops down for a moment, flies off over the hedge as if panicked by something we haven't seen. He shakes his head slowly, like it's suddenly too heavy to move. He picks at his scone, throws crumbs on to the ground. 'She'll be back,' he says. 'The little wren.'

He draws up his muddy knees, rests his head on them. 'He lost his job,' he says. 'Got laid off. Back last summer. And now it's like he's lost himself too. Bit like your mam. Only he did know who he was, and now he's forgotten.' He pushes his hands through his hair, knots his fingers together behind his neck, like he has to force out the next words.

'At the start, he was out there, looking for work every day. Still making things too. His art and stuff. Shell mosaics. Sea-glass wind chimes and dreamcatchers for Maggie's gift shop. Paintings of the sea. He was still Dad.' His voice wobbles. He buries his chin further into his knees. I have to bend forward to hear. 'Since Christmas,' he says, 'he hardly gets out of bed half the time. It's like he's forgetting me too. Forgetting I'm even there.'

He stares off into the distance, into wherever it is he goes to escape.

'I'm sorry,' I say. I hesitate, unsure whether to fill the space with my own words in case he needs it for his own. 'So that's why you've been doing all this – the gardening, shopping, and stuff . . .'

He's back. There's a flash of wild sea behind his glasses.

'I thought if I just kept things going for a bit, he'd get better. Get rested, find himself again.' He shakes his head. 'But he's just, letting me do it. All of it. Cooking, washing. Collecting things . . . beautiful things that might bring him back, like before.' His voice creaks and cracks like it's old and tired and doesn't belong to a Beach-Bird-Boy who's not much older than me. 'Nothing. None of it works. And now . . .' He swallows hard. Then he shakes his head, pushes the rest of the scone into his mouth and brushes crumbs from his hands like he's brushing away his thoughts too.

'Isn't there someone?' I say. 'Someone who could help? Your mam – does she know?'

'We'll be OK,' Freddie says, getting to his feet. There's a wish – and a full stop – in his words that tells me he doesn't know how to make them true. That he feels all alone too. And *he* doesn't even have a brother waiting for him. 'Come on, work to do, Jonah,' he says. 'Strawberry plants next.'

CHAPTER 30

Silence stretches between us as we work. Freddie bends low over the soil, stares into his newly dug holes and empties pots like he might find the help he needs there. And maybe there's a kind of magic in the touch of the soil, the rhythm of the work, because after a while, he finds his voice again, just like I did. He keeps his eyes down, lets his words fall in among the tangle of roots and earth, because this time they hold the worst of it and he might need to cover them, quick-sharp.

A letter came this morning, he tells me, landed on the mat like a cruel red and white bird. He and his dad, they're losing their home. The one Freddie's lived in since he was born. The one where his mam once lived. The only home he's ever known. And even though I've never had a proper home and don't know what it feels like to stay in one place longer than memories, this is Freddie's Whitby sea-storm and it can wash everything important away. I know how that feels. In spades.

It's called 'getting evicted' and it's because they can't afford the rent any more, haven't been able to pay it, even with money from the Social. Which, like Mam said, makes you choose between having food in your bellies and coins for the electric, or keeping the landlord from the door. Freddie's tried everything. That's what the beach-bird behaviour's about, the scouring the sand for things that wink and glint and gleam. Finding things to sell. Things that might tempt his dad's hands to make things again: to thread the hidden sea treasures on to wire, see them twist and turn and dance in the light, singing with the wind. Catching dreams and chasing nightmares clean away.

None of it has worked and Freddie's tired, tired, tired. He fell asleep in Ms Mukherjee's class twice last week and she knows something's up and if they find out about Dad, what then?

Which they will. When he and Dad are homeless, looking for shelter in the caves, like the fox. He throws an empty plant pot high in the air. It hits the shed door, shatters into pink shards, painting red-scribble feelings all over the grey gravel path.

So Freddie has them too. Freddie with his stillness and his open-sky face. Open-sky heart. And it's not because he's bad. Or bad luck to be around. It's because he needs to save someone, but he's lost in a maze and doesn't know the way out.

It's because he cares.

Because he is afraid.

Freddie, the Beach-Bird Boy that dances with my fox, he's just like me. And he's my friend.

So I tell him. About Grandad Ted's box and the maps and the pizza-coin clue, and the smugglers' stash waiting to be found somewhere deep in the cliff leading from the fox's cave. Because he needs it too. Because we can share.

That's what friends do.

'We'll find it together,' I say. 'Then we'll all be OK. You and your dad, me and Rio. Maybe even our mam. And if Mimi's right, and there's some stupid rules that says finders can't be keepers when it's famous treasure, there'll still be a reward. There will. And it will be HUGE . . . it has to be. Huge enough for two homes.'

Freddie looks unsure for a moment. My blood thunders in my ears. Have I made a mistake? Got it wrong *again*?

Then he nods. 'Thank you, Jonah,' he says. And his eyes spark like sea diamonds, and they are small green seas, safe and kind and honest. He hooks his little finger around mine, like Rio does, promises not to tell. And *this* promise feels real and clear, set in stone like an ammonite.

'Right,' he says. 'Mission on.'

Arthur is back and so is his wheelbarrow. He waves, nods at the newly planted beds, holds up his thumb. 'Nice job, lads,' he calls. 'Plenty to do here if you want more practice.' He laughs loud enough to shake the new buds from the trees and even the birds fall silent. He's still looking over, leaning on a rake now.

'C'mon into the shed,' Freddie says. 'Give old Arthur half a chance and he'll be over chatting till the moon's up. And if he hears anything interesting, everyone else in the town will hear it by tomorrow.'

The shed is warm and smells like Christmas trees. The real sort that Jo has. We sit on upturned boxes and eat the rest of Mimi's food, hungry now that our insides aren't clogged up with a rockfall of sharp-edged words. We put our heads together, whisper our plans like smugglers in their den. We need to act soon. Before Rio is taken, before the bailiffs turn up at Freddie's house with their monster van and new locks to bar Freddie and his dad from their home, steal their memories away.

But we need to be careful. We need to go in daylight. Even though it won't help us once we enter the smugglers' maze, neither of us want to brave Boggle Hole, its stony, slippery cove, sudden rockfalls, and swirling tides, in the middle of the night.

I wait for Freddie to talk about checking the sky for ancient signs – which he does – but as I open my mouth to splutter about tide tables and weather stations and science, he pulls his phone from his pocket and columns of numbers and dates flash on to the blue screen.

'Tuesday,' he says. 'Look.' He points, rubs soil smudges from the glass. 'Clear, dry, tide won't come in until nine thirty-ish. High moon rising. Perfect. But after that, there's a week of "unsettled" weather; rain and wind and who knows what round here. If we don't go Tuesday, we'll be waiting a while. Too long.'

'What about school?' I say. 'You can't just bunk off, can you? Not with – what's her name, Ms Mukherjee on your case . . .'

'Inset day,' Freddie says. 'See? Meant to be.' His eyes look into mine, burning bright, like the fox's golden stare. 'You bring your maps and clues, a torch of your own, and thick clothes – it's cold underground. And lose the wellies,' he says, his mouth sliding into a sideways grin. 'They'll slow you down.'

'Right,' I say. And my insides fizz and jump like firecrackers because we're DOING this. Three days from now. But as I wander back to Mimi's house, something cold is creeping around the base of my stomach, trying to douse the flames; our plan – *my* plan – it's dangerous. Desperate. No one will know where to find us if we get lost down there. Will someone find our bones one day, bleached white like the rabbit bones left by the fox?

What if there IS no smugglers' stash, and it's all for nothing? What if Rio thinks I've left him on purpose, just like Mam?

The sun is suddenly blinding, red as fire above the cottage roofs. I feel the lift of the dream fox, see the burn of her eyes. And I remember. She came to tell me.

I am brave and I can do this. This is going to WORK.

I didn't see her today. And maybe that's because her job is done. I hope not; we're part of one another now. And I need longer for my new brave self to take root. But I smile as I open Mimi's front door, tug at my wellies on the mat, hear her happy feet clattering downstairs to greet me. Quite possibly the most difficult thing about our mission will be getting past Mimi without these stupid boots.

CHAPTER 31

I spend Sunday pouring over Grandad Ted's maze map, making a sketch of it, because Mimi trusted me with the original, and if it gets spoiled or lost in the tunnels it will be like part of him is spoiled or lost too. I tell her it's so I can share the smugglers' story with Rio, that he loves anything to do with treasure and pirates, and smugglers are nearly the same, aren't they? She looks pleased to see me engrossed, and being excited about my drawings is good camouflage in case her X-ray vision is working. She finds tissue-thin paper, and I trace over the pizza-shaped piece of eight with a soft pencil, scribble and press its image into my notebook.

I sort through the clothes I still keep in my suitcase, putting jumpers and sweatshirts into drawers with the warmest ones on top, ready for Tuesday. I take the new grey coat Jo bought me from its bag for the first time, try it on. It's soft and warm and light, and it's a coat like a hug that will make me feel safer in the damp, dark tunnel maze.

A coat you buy for someone you care about. Like Rio's Paddington coat that has room for him to grow into himself.

'Very organised, pet. Well done,' Mimi says.

And then my room feels like another lie, like I'm calling this home, giving in. The snakes crawl back, wriggling and winding inside me. But when Freddie and me find Grandad Ted's treasure, we'll be bringing part of him home too. Maybe that will smooth the edges off the lies because something precious was waiting to be found inside them.

Freddie rings on Monday morning, His voice is a thin whisper inside Mimi's massive telephone speaker. He's ready. For the mission. He asks to speak to Mimi, and another lie travels down the phone line into her home, spreads a smile that stabs at my heart. He's phoned to invite me to lunch tomorrow. Twelve noon by the coastguard 'castle', so we can hunt for fossils and jet. It's going to be a beautiful day. No need for wellies. And thank you, Mimi, for the Saturday cheese scones. They were the best ever.

I think how phones can hide lies, make people a master of disguise, like the amazing creatures at the bottom of the sea. Freddie's eyes are as clear as rainwater. If Mimi could see them, she'd know. I hope our mission succeeds, and Freddie doesn't have to keep lying and get good at hiding things like me.

But the Monday sky looks like it's getting ready for our mission too. It's summer blue. Clouds drift past the window like white party balloons and there's something new and light inside me, pushing for space beside the worrying. Perhaps it's hope.

Mimi's bought a bird table in a box for her tiny garden. It's like a puzzle made of wood and it feels good to help her bring the pieces together, fix it in the branches of the bent cherry tree by the back gate ready for a bird family to move in. It makes the day seem quieter, settles the churning in my stomach as the clock ticks round towards Tuesday, twelve noon.

Mimi's mobile rings, rips a hole in the peaceful day. It's Not-Nadia, asking if I'd like to meet Amos and Sam, Rio's adopters, on Friday. Before Rio moves in with them. ONE WEEK.

Two dads. If I don't stop it, Rio's going to be like the 'window children' near Mimi's street. I'll be outside in the rain, nose against the glass, and his dads will close the curtains like I'm not even there . . .

No.

The churning and the lies and the danger don't matter any more. Tuesday can't come soon enough. Bring it on.

Mimi goes for a bath, and I collect everything I need for the next morning, put it into my backpack. Map and tracing. My notebook. Torch. A bottle of water from the fridge. Two packets of peanuts and apples from the bowl, because I'm allowed to help myself to those. Two chocolate bars, a chunk of cheese that Mimi says is too strong, and half a packet of digestive biscuits from the back of the cupboard that hopefully she's forgotten about. She'll notice the chocolate bars are missing, but they'll be down inside the Boggle Hole cliff with me and Freddie by then, so I think I'm safe. I find a ball of string under the sink and add that because it looks useful, and a handful of plasters in case the sharp cliff face fights back like last time.

I lie on my bed, watch moon shadows play on the ceiling, listen to Mimi's snores, wait for the slide of the Tuesday sun.

CHAPTER 32

The sound whines like a Word War Two siren, splits my sleep like an electric shock. I jolt upright, one foot in a dream I didn't know I'd been having and I'm cold-shower awake in a second.

Outside my window, the fox is a twisting red flag under the streetlamp. She's circling like panic. She stops, stretches out her neck and the sound comes again. Eerie. Ear-splitting.

EMERGENCY.

EMERGENCY . . .

I open the window and a stiff wind wraps around my head like an icy towel, the sun's warmth forgotten for now. Early fog drifts in tumbleweed clumps in the street. No sign yet of Freddie's calm, clear Tuesday.

The fox sits, stares, like one of those sniffer dogs that freezes when it finds its target.

She needs me to come. And in that moment, I know.

This is something to do with Freddie. He needs me.

I've no idea how to speak fox – and I daren't call out. So I raise both hands, like I used to do when I wanted Milo to wait. I slide around the room in my socks; slide open my drawers and dress in thick layers, alert for Mimi's soft knock and ready to dive back under the covers at any moment.

She *must* have heard the fox.

She doesn't come. Her room is at the back, over the garden, and perhaps the wind is blowing the siren call in the other direction. Which means it's blowing off the sea.

What if it's blowing in the tide? I check my clock. 5 a.m.

It's definitely Tuesday now. This is starting to feel like the *wrong* Tuesday.

The fox calls again. I rush to the window.

'I'm coming,' I whisper-shout. I grab my backpack, because wherever we're going, I might need it.

Wherever we're going, I'm heading straight for the caves and our mission once I've found out what the fuss is all about.

The fox sprints away the moment I step on to the pavement. I glance up at the house and my held breath explodes like smoke on the air. No sudden-bright windows. So much for Mimi the light sleeper. I can only hope

I'm back before she does wake or she's going to feel terrible. Feel afraid for me.

The fox leaps up and down, barks, races off again once she's sure I'm following. Her feet fly, picking up speed on the tilting streets, and she is the wind. I run behind her, eyes fixed on the white tip of her disappearing tail as she bends and twists with the wonky streets, swerves around corners. My breath scrapes and rasps. My blood drums danger in my ears.

We're heading for the beach.

The fox waits at the slipway, silhouetted under the last of the streetlamps. My feet slow; drag. The darkness stretches away towards the sea, where waves lift and fall like silver serpents under the moonlight. Are they advancing or retreating? I can't tell. Looks like they're not sure, either. Arguing about it. Angry.

I try to get a sense of how far back they are, but the dark is a trickster. I can't tell. I need Freddie and his sea senses. Because the tide tables and weather sites: looks like they lied.

The fox howls again and the wind steals the sound. I've no choice but to keep going.

She swings left. Left, round the ship's-hull bend in the cliff face.

Left, towards Boggle Hole.

My heart batters my ribcage and the moon is a spotlight on the sea. A spotlight on danger.

Freddie is at the cave. I just *know* it.

My feet pound on the damp, compacted sand. Surely he isn't trying to get to the smugglers' stash before me. He wouldn't. Not Freddie. He's my friend.

But then, why . . .?

Has the fox brought me to catch him out? But no. My senses flare like the fox is in me. Whatever the reason, Freddie is in that cave and he's in danger. He needs us. And fast.

Sand turns to shale and the moon swoops lower. I scan for the rise of the sun, but it's a no-show, hiding its face like it can't bear to look.

The fox keeps turning to check I'm still there. Her eyes are yellow traffic lights in the darkness: stop-start-stop. Like my heartbeat.

The beach is rockier now. My feet struggle worse than before on sea-spray washed slabs, lying like sleeping whales under my feet. We're close.

And so is the sea. I'm sure of it.

I flick on my torch because Freddie will be here, strolling towards us, and I've just been Jonah that worries too much again. But there *is* no Freddie. Just a giant-sized black shadow-fox in the torchlight, running, running, running on the stony face of the cliff . . .

We're here. The fox circles round and round, leaps on and off the boulder marker at the cave. Up and down the craggy cliff-face climb to the opening. She's saying come ON, come ON, emergency, emergency: follow me. NOW, NOW. NOW.

I hold my torch in my teeth and make my too-heavy feet climb towards her. The rock is slip-slide wet already and I'm scared, scared, scared. How much time do we have? I try to listen for the sea like Freddie says, but my blood is roaring too loud in my ears.

I s t r e t c h forward, poke my head inside the drip-drip silence of the cave. The cold grabs my face. The fox squeezes past me. Her claws scritch-scratch on the floor like a hundred rats. The roar in my ears is louder and I don't know if it's the sea now or maybe the wind or just my own blood.

I want Mimi with her purple boots and her bossy ways and her taking care of things. But there's just me and the fox and I have to keep being Jonah the Brave.

I call out.

'FREDDIE . . .'

'FREDDIE ...'

My voice bounces off the stone walls:

'Freddie.

'Freddie ... Freddie ... Freddie.'

No reply.

Best not shout any more, because in films that makes stones fall and ceilings collapse, and people get buried alive. That might be true in the real world too.

I remember about the soldiers sliding through the tunnels, their muskets silent at their sides, and I know that it is.

CHAPTER 33

The fox rushes down into the first tunnel, the one with the piece-of-eight marker. She's fluid, like water in the beam from my torch, moving easily in the tight space. When she turns, her eyes glare at me, unblinking. She is panting, her breathing dragon-loud in the echoey tunnel.

There's a rushing in my ears which might be my blood. But could be the sea, roaring its way towards the cave. Only the fox wouldn't get herself trapped like that. Or me. Foxes are wise and wily.

I need to trust her.

I push my backpack ahead of me, wriggle inside on my stomach, biting back terror and trying to remember to breathe. There's a hollow sound, like when your ears go funny riding up a steep hill in the car, or when they're blocked with the worst cold ever and it's like your head might explode.

The tunnel winds like a snake, divides again. This time into three. The fox pauses, waits for me, disappears down the second one and a thousand butterflies fluster in my stomach. My throat is terror tight. I direct my torch inside, dazzling the fox and making her sneeze like an explosion.

This tunnel widens out, its roof rounding a little higher above her head. I take some deep breaths, trying not to think about how much oxygen there might be this deep inside the cliff. Trying not to think about being deep inside the cliff at all.

And I see them. Just inside the tunnel's mouth, like before. Only this time, there are two. Two pizza-slice triangles carved into the rock, picked out in the yellow beam.

Another clue!

I'm going the right way for the smugglers' stash. Hope leaps again. Because Grandad Ted's smugglers' maze has an escape route. The one the smugglers took after they'd hidden their haul. So if the sea IS following . . .

If I'm right, if Freddie is down here, he'll have spotted the clues with his bird-sharp eyes. He'll have gone this way.

I let the fox lead on.

And on . . . her body snake-supple as she twists and turns with the tunnel.

Another tunnel branches off. I circle my torch around its oval, green-stained mouth. Three pieces of eight this time . . .

We're on the trail. We *really* are.

But where's Freddie?

The base of the next tunnel is drier. Dust fills my nostrils and panic rises as the fox's feet kick back tiny stones that dig into my hands and knees as I crawl. Round a sharp, dog-leg bend, light spills. The fox is pushing at something with her nose. Something that rolls towards me, bringing the light with it.

A torch.

Freddie's torch with the silver handle.

I speed-crawl around the bend, ignoring the sting of gravel in my palms, the dust clouds behind the fox's urgent feet. I risk a whispered call. My rasping voice repeats and repeats and repeats, quieter each time.

No reply.

For a moment, I lose the fox, panic blindly in the direction of the dust clouds.

A cave within a cave. A round space anyway.

The fox, still. Her white chest and tail grey with dust.

Next to her, slumped against the cave wall: Freddie, his clothes, his skin, pale as plaster. Like he's a mummy from long ago. His glasses wink in the torchlight. But he's still, chin on chest.

Fear strangles me. Is he even alive?

'Freddie,' I whisper. 'FREDDIE.'

His head lifts, clockwork-slow. The fox is licking his face, his neck. Her tail wags, stirs the dusty air.

'Jonah,' Freddie croaks. 'How . . .?'

'The fox,' I say, crawling close. 'She came for me . . .'

I scan his body. One of his boots is off, lying beside him. 'What are you doing here . . .? Why . . .? I don't get it.'

He winces. 'My ankle,' he says. 'Broken or . . .'

But there's no time for more. No time for broken bones, clues or treasure-hunting. No time for blame or apologies. There's just a mighty roar, like a hundred sea monsters are hurtling through the maze towards us, hairs standing like spiked armour on the fox's neck and panic filling the cave.

I know that sound. I've heard it in my nightmares. So much for science and tide tables.

A long-ago sea carved these tunnels.

Today's sea is taking them back.

The fox is circling like crazy. Her unearthly scream ricochets around us.

'Go, Jonah,' Freddie says. 'Now. While you still can. She'll get you out somehow. She'll know . . .'

I grab at his arm, my grip like foxes' teeth. 'Come on,' I say. 'I'm not leaving you.'

He struggles to his knees, tries to stand. 'I knew,' he mutters. 'Felt it. The sea. This. Stupid,' he says. A sob escapes, fills the cave.

I drape his arm over my shoulder, half drag him to the next tunnel. His foot twists behind him in the dust. I push and shove him with a strength I didn't know I had, down the next tunnel as the roaring beasts grow louder. Closer at our heels. Covers Freddie's stifled cries of pain.

The fox has stopped. Her tongue lies over the side of her mouth. She might be smiling.

Has she found the way out?

She's not smiling. Neither are we as we twist around the next bend.

A HUGE pile of rocks and stones blocks our way. The fox leaps from stone to stone.

This is the way. The way through to town. She's frantic. She's out of options. And so are we.

We're all trapped. Sitting ducks for the surging, suffocating sea.

Freddie collapses, head in hands. 'My fault,' he says. 'All my fault. I'm so sorry, Jonah. I knew . . . I sensed it. This sea. This freak tide.' He shakes his head. 'And then

I checked the tables again, and it was THERE: WARNING. WARNING. FREAK HIGH TIDE ALERT.' He chokes back a sob. 'I just wanted to try . . . for both of us. I thought I had time . . .'

I stare at him. At the fox, furiously digging at the rockfall barrier, sending stone arrows, dust and debris high into the stuffy air. I heave one of the larger stones out of the way. Reach for another. 'You should have called me,' I hiss. 'Asked me. This was MY idea. MY mission. For Rio.'

He shakes his head. 'I wanted you to be safe,' he says. 'I thought . . . I thought I could do it . . .' His voice breaks. 'I wasn't trying to take it for myself, Jonah. The reward. I wouldn't . . .'

'I know,' I say. 'I . . .'

But the sea's roar steals my voice. Froth licks the dusty floor.

'We're all getting out,' I say. 'Watch yourself. Sit on that big stone,' I yell. 'Wait . . .'

If he heard me, he's not listening. He's beside me, on his knees, pulling at the bigger stones, his face a puzzle of pain.

I pull a T-shirt from my bag, wrap it around my nose and mouth. I dig alongside the fox, alongside my friend. My hands are blood red, and I am the fox and the fox is me, Jonah the Brave.

Digging for Rio.
For my friend Freddie.
Digging for my life.

CHAPTER 34

There's a door. Green with moss and mould, the old wooden slats held together by rusted metal bands. The fox is on her hind legs, scratching and scraping at it with her claws, making long white stripes on the soft wood. We lean our shoulders, our whole weight against it – and it gives, opens. Drags against the stone floor. We squeeze round it just as a huge wave rushes in, lifting the rockfall debris, flinging it in the air like an angry toddler tired of its toys.

The noise is deafening. Thunder. We press our backs to the door, press it shut. But how long can it hold against the weight of water on the other side?

Does the sea have anywhere else to go?

Our torches. They're on the other side of the door. The darkness wraps around us, thick as tar.

The fox yips. A rough tongue touches my hand.

I feel forward with the toe of my trainer. It hits something solid.

Please no. Not another roadblock.

My eyes adjust a little. Another excited yip. The white tip of the fox's tail moves high in the air.

Higher still.

I bend forward.

STEPS. Stone steps. I feel around with my hands. The white tail flag waves at me.

'Stairs,' I yell over the deafening roar from behind the door. 'She's climbing stairs. QUICK. Follow her.'

And we do. Freddie on all fours, like the fox. She runs up and down, up and down, hurrying us both. Nudging Freddie's bottom with her nose.

The stairs twist and turn like the tunnel. Up, up, up, rising like the steep streets out in the town. Up, up, up we stumble, leaving behind the reaching fingers and angry voice of the ocean.

Another door. This one full of holes and swinging open on one hinge. It groans as we push though and collapse on the cold floor beyond it.

Stone. Hard cold stone again. But these are flagstones, lit by slices of moonlight through narrow slit windows. A large, round barrel is shadowed on the wall.

'A cellar?' I say.

I look at Freddie. His face is paler than the moonlight. And it's not dust. It's pain.

The fox is still, lit by the moon, her silhouette spreading up the first steps of another staircase. Her eyes fix on me like a collie controlling a sheep. Her head turns, her shoulders sink low, her nose points. She lifts one paw. Looks upwards. This way, she's saying. Just this one last bit, and you're free . . .

'Thank you,' I say. 'We're coming . . . good girl . . .'

Freddie is shaking his head. 'I can't,' he says. 'Can't . . .'

He fumbles in his soaked jeans pocket. Brings out his phone.

I stare at him. 'No way! You had this, all the time?'

'No signal underground,' he whispers. 'Take it. Ring . . .'

His eyes droop, and panic pushes me up the steps. Out through a small, square room, empty except for a carpet of dust and leaves, and a family of pigeons roosting on the back of a broken chair.

Out through a doorway with no door . . . and my tears are a hot river of relief as Freddie's blue-star phone shines like home in the shuttered window of George's Bakery – shines bigger, better, brighter than all the sea diamonds, all the smugglers' spoils in the wide, wild world.

CHAPTER 35

I'm wrapped in yellow blankets, like a fat banana in a hospital cubicle. My teeth keep chitter-chattering. Mimi has hot chocolate in a flask, but the nurse says I'm not allowed it yet. I have to warm up slowly. Freddie is a banana too, in X-Ray. I peer round the curtain. 'What's taking so long?'

'He'll not be much longer now, pet,' Mimi says. 'Doctor thinks it's a nasty sprain, not a break. It'll cramp his style for a while, but he'll be OK.' She rests her hand on my arm. 'His dad's with him,' she says. 'They've a lot to talk about.'

I nod.

'Your social worker's on her way,' she says.

My stomach goes tight, and it must show in my face because she strokes wet hair back from it.

'She had to know, Jonah,' she says.

I bite my lip. 'Rules,' I say. 'Yes.'

I glance at the loud black numbers on the hospital clock. It's not even seven in the morning yet. If Not-Nadia's coming out this early, I'm in even more trouble than I thought.

'But that was a very brave thing that you did, Jonah,' Mimi is saying. 'She knows that.'

I shake my head. 'It wasn't,' I say, trying to steady my teeth. 'I was scared. Really scared the whole time. And *I* didn't rescue Freddie. *Or* save myself. The fox did.'

Mimi smiles. I'm not sure she believes me about the fox. She shot away long before the whine of the ambulance reached my ears. Although I'm sure I caught a flash of red-gold from behind a bin, just as Mimi's blue bubble car screeched to a halt by George's, and the man who could only be Freddie's dad fell into the street from the passenger seat.

But where will she go – now that her cave is flooded? She should be here, drinking warm milk, being welcomed like the hero she is.

Mimi is still talking. 'You *were* brave, lad,' she says. 'Very brave indeed. That's what "brave" means: being afraid but doing the thing you're scared of anyway.'

Her eyes are soft, serious. 'You've had to be brave a great deal, Jonah, in your short life. Too much. Too often . . . and in too many ways.' She tips up my chin with her finger. 'You're awesome. I'm proud of you.'

She drags her chair closer to my bed. 'Trying to rescue your friend like you did, that was a beautiful thing. But it wasn't the *right* thing to do. Not for a ten-year-old boy. Not even for most grown-ups. A sea-cave rescue: that needs specially trained grown-ups, special equipment. I think you know that really, don't you?'

I look down into my yellow lap. 'Freddie,' I say. 'He was there because of me. It was my idea . . .'

Mimi shakes her head. 'Freddie's dad and I, we've had a chat,' she says. 'I know how things have been.' She sighs. 'I just wish they'd spoken out; asked for help. But easier said than done, often.' She takes my hand in hers and I think of Rio's hand, folded inside my own like a smooth shell, sticky with something always. I don't remember anyone else holding mine. Not till now.

'Freddie was there because he's brave too,' Mimi goes on. 'And because he's kind and caring and – and a worrier, just like you. But Freddie knows better than you that this was NOT a sensible thing to do. Freddie knows the sea. And as I believe his dad is telling him right now, it's not his job to rescue his family or save their home. That's for grown-ups too.'

She pauses, fixes my eyes with her own and they're fox eyes. Wise, and full of fire. 'Just like it's not your job to rescue Rio or take care of him all the time.

'And you know what, Jonah,' she says. 'He doesn't need rescuing. Not any more. He has a safe home with two dads that have chosen him; dads that are going to love and protect him, like he deserves.'

'I just wanted everyone to see,' I say. Mimi waits. 'That I'm a good big brother. The best. That I can be a good example. That we can be together. I wanted them to see that I'm not messed-up Bad-Luck Jonah any more.'

My eyes overflow again, like since the river broke through, there's no holding it back now. My plan failed. I let Rio down. If the smugglers' stash even existed, the sea has stolen it away again.

'I have to make a home for Rio and me,' I sob. 'And then, and then . . . and then, maybe Mam will come home.'

Mimi's voice is gentle and firm as the wind. 'You have nothing to prove, Jonah. You never did have. Everyone has always known you're the best big brother anyone could have. THE BEST.' She wipes tears from my cheek with her thumb. 'And no one – no one is going to stop you being a big part of Rio's life. But you need to learn to be just Jonah too. Jonah who is ten (nearly eleven) and who loves fossils and drawing and finding out things. Jonah who speaks "wild fox". Jonah who has the biggest heart in the world. Jonah who needs to let grown-ups look after *him* for once.

'Rio has that now,' she says. 'And his new dads want to make sure you're a big part of their forever family, if you'll let them. You'll see. That's why they've insisted they meet you even before Rio moves in for good.

'So, it's your turn, Jonah.

'And that,' she says, unscrewing the lid on her famous hot chocolate. 'That's where I come in. If you'll have me. Me and "Not-Nadia", or whatever you like to call her. Lucky us.' She beams at me. 'And we'll start with a nice bit of home, shall we?' She checks over her shoulder for the nurse, hands me a steaming cup. 'Must be OK now, surely. Blow on it first, though . . .'

EPILOGUE

The July sun spins gold in Rio's curls as he races across the sand, his Paddington coat flapping behind him like sails.

He won't take it off, even though he must be way too warm. He's inches taller already. 'Like he's been planted in the right soil,' Freddie says.

I watch his new dad, Amos, lift him in the air above the waves, high as the moon, and I smile. That coat will soon be too small. Good luck to Amos and Sam persuading Rio to wear something else.

Freddie and I hold tiny paper boats. Mine has rainbow-striped sails. Folded inside are messages. Mine is for Mam.

It says it's OK if she's lost her way. That I hope she finds her way home. That me and Rio are fine. That we love her.

I don't know what Freddie wrote. But his eyes were gentle as he folded his words away and shaped the hull around them.

The waves run soft over our feet. We bend, set the boats free. We sit on the sand, chins on our knees, and watch them bob on the waves like birds; let the sea take them.

I think of the fox, scan the bay for her like always. But she won't be there, I know that. She's already said her goodbyes.

She came on the first night of July, slipping out of the darkness, calling under my window one last time. Eyes like twin moons. Her belly round and full and fat – a new family of her own hidden inside like secret diamonds.

We walk back up the beach together, all headed to Mimi's for tea and scones and another of Lois's 'speciality' cakes. Sam will have his guitar in the car. Freddie has a surprise for Rio, hidden in the room we're sharing while his dad gets back on his feet again.

It's a dreamcatcher. Made from emerald sea glass and pearl-white shells that clink and sing to keep him company in the night; tell sea stories of their own.

Rio runs towards me, waving a huge stick in the air. He holds it out to me.

I write our names in the sand. I draw a huge heart around them. By morning, they will be gone.

But that's OK. Because wherever we go, whatever happens, we're always part of one another.

Jonah, Rio, Freddie.

And the smugglers' fox.

ACKNOWLEDGEMENTS

In telling Jonah and Rio's story, my thoughts lay with the many amazing Looked-After siblings in whose lives I briefly shared as fostering and adoption social worker, and with all young people currently separated from someone they love, or feeling lost and afraid like Jonah, Rio and Freddie. May they all, like Jonah, find a true friend, and come to know that they are enough, just as they are.

Thank you to Sue Carter, who kindly shared her own insights into siblings in the current Care system, and to all those who are truly there for children and families, working to help each of them through their own particular maze within an imperfect, under-resourced, system.

Very special thanks also to:

Keith Robinson, for his stunning, atmospheric cover illustration that so sensitively captures the story setting, and the relationship between Jonah and his fox. (You have him, Keith: my Jonah. Right there. I have no idea how you do that!)

The editorial team at Farshore, especially Asmaa Isse, who helped me polish this manuscript so that the children's voices could truly shine through. The Design and Marketing teams, and everyone else involved in bringing *Smugglers' Fox* out into the daylight . . .

As always, to my lovely agent Emily Talbot. Your support and expertise keep me afloat in the uncertain waters of being an author. I am so lucky to have you in my corner. Thanks, too, to Molly Jamieson, for looking after me in your absence.

Most of all, my love and thanks to my beautiful children and grandchildren. Oceans may separate some of us, but you are all here, right at the centre of everything, every day. The greatest treasure imaginable.

AUTHOR NOTES

Robin Hood's Bay and Whitby are real places, near where I grew up in North Yorkshire. I have changed one or two things about these places to make Jonah and Rio's story work. But most of the things that Jonah encounters exist in the area.

The origin of the name **Robin Hood's Bay** is intriguing. Local legend has it that the name was given in gratitude, after Robin Hood visited the town, defeated French pirates, and returned loot stolen from poor local families and fishermen. Its true origins remain a mystery.

But smugglers really did frequent the bay, getting up to all kinds of skulduggery in tunnels, caves, and hideouts in the town. There might well be treasures stashed away in the cliff-face or at the bottom of the ocean, waiting to be found. Who knows?

Whitby has fascinating history, dating back to the Bronze Age. It provided author Bram Stoker with settings and characters for his famous Gothic novel – and a name for its dastardly vampire protagonist, Count Dracula.

A FEW FOX FACTS

Jonah's fox is a red fox, the most common
of the twelve fox species.

Foxes are part of the canine (dog) family
and related to wolves.

They can be found on almost every continent.

They have supersonic hearing: they can hear insects
scuttling underground and a watch ticking
from over 36 metres away.

They have vertical pupils, like a cat. This helps
them see in the dark, which is when they do most of
their hunting and scavenging.

Foxes will eat pretty much anything,
from berries and spiders to the contents of
household food bins – even cakes and
jam sandwiches.

They do not hibernate, but shelter from the
worst winter weather.

They can run at speeds of up to 30 miles per hour.

Foxes use 28 different calls when communicating
with their mates.

They have inspired legend, story, poems, and other forms
of art across the ages and across much of the world.
(Can you think of any examples?)

HELP AND SUPPORT FOR
ALL CHILDREN AND YOUNG PEOPLE

Childline gives children and young people a voice when no one else is listening. Whatever problems or dangers they face, whatever their worries, they give them somewhere to turn for support when they need it.

Childline is free to contact and counsellors are there seven days a week to take calls from young people under the age of nineteen.

If you can't call, there are a number of other ways to contact Childline, either in an emergency, or if you need other, ongoing help/ways to manage your feelings. Look online to find all of this information and step-by-step guides to using the service.

LOOKED-AFTER CHILDREN AND YOUNG PEOPLE

Coram Voices is an organisation set up to ensure that the voices of Looked-After Children are heard.

Their **'Always Heard'** service provides advice and advocacy for Looked-After Children, Care Leavers, and young people on the edge of care from 0 to 25 years old.

Their website explains how Looked-After Children can be supported by an Advocate: someone who is 'always on your side' in whatever is happening. It explains the role of an advocate, and how to find one near you. You can contact the helpline for free.

Complete your collection today!

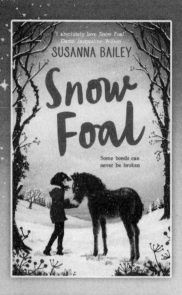

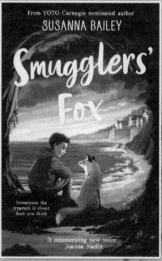